TALES FOR THE MIDNIGHT HOUR

Stories Of Horror
J.B. Stamper

SCHOLASTIC INC.
New York Toronto London Auckland Sydney

Other Scholastic paperbacks
by J.B. STAMPER:

More Tales for the Midnight Hour
Still More Tales for the Midnight Hour
Even More Tales for the Midnight Hour

ISBN 0-590-45343-2

36 35 34 33 32 31 30 29 28 27   25   11 12 13 14/0

Printed in the U.S.A.

CONTENTS

A full moon is in the sky,
The clock strikes twelve ...
These are tales for the midnight hour!

THE FURRY COLLAR

Susan was my best friend. But I try never to think about her. It's only on certain nights, when I'm all alone in my room, that I remember...

It was during Christmas vacation last year when Susan asked me to stay at her house overnight. She lived in a big, gloomy house set way back from the road. And she didn't want to be alone there at night. Her parents had gone to visit some friends and wouldn't be back until the next afternoon. Susan said we could have a really good time without her parents around.

And we did. At about 12:00 we decided to get dressed for bed. Susan had gotten this velvet nightrobe for Christmas that had a thick furry collar. It was blood red velvet and she looked like someone from a Dracula movie in it. We had been watching television in the living room, but then we turned it off. We hadn't noticed it before, but now the downstairs seemed too big, and almost sinister.

We started to go upstairs. Then, all of a sudden, we both ran up the steps to Susan's room as if something was coming up from behind us. After we closed the door, we laughed at ourselves. But neither one of us wanted to leave the room again. We sat down and started to talk. That's when we first heard the noise. It sounded like somebody sharpening a knife on an old emery stone.

We stopped talking and looked at each other, feeling really scared inside. There was just a thick silence in the room. Suddenly, Susan started to laugh. She said she had heard a sound like that in the house before. She said it was probably the shutters or something. That made me feel better and we started to talk again. Then we heard it again! SCRRITCH. SCRRITCH. The sound made my teeth vibrate as if somebody's fingernails were scratching on a chalkboard. But this sound was much worse. It shrieked up from the dark, lonely rooms below us. SCRRITCH.

Susan got a wild look in her eyes, as though something horrible had come into her head. Before I could catch her, she ran out of the room, slamming the door shut and flicking off the light switch. I heard her footsteps as she ran down the first flight of stairs, and then stop.

I sat in the dark, sick with fright. I called out Susan's name; but my voice was answered by hushed silence. I didn't want to stay in the dark room alone, but even more I didn't want to go out into that other darkness. SCRRITCH.

I heard it again, that disgusting sound. Then I heard Susan's footsteps, moving down the next and final flight of stairs. She went more slowly, as if she really didn't want to. I heard her reach the bottom. I waited in the room, wondering what Susan was doing. I told myself she must be all right. You see, the noise had stopped right after I heard her reach the bottom of the stairs. It didn't come after that. Susan had probably just fixed the shutter. Maybe she had known for sure about that all the time. She had just acted strangely to scare me. Maybe she was sitting on the steps now, laughing at me.

I got up and started toward the door to turn the light on. But a feeling of fear swept over me that held me back like a hand against my throat. I decided I would wait where I was for Susan to return. I would wait there until her parents returned, if necessary. Nothing could make me leave my darkness for that darker unknown outside the room.

Time passed. My ears strained for a sound and my nerves tingled at imagined shadows. Then I heard a slow, shuffling noise on the bottom step. Was it Susan? It had to be. Yet the footsteps seemed too heavy, too deliberate. My heart began to pound and for a moment I lost control of my mind. It flew to the most horrible corners of my imagination and I shook with terror.

Then, suddenly, I knew what I would do. Susan's new nightrobe with the furry collar! I would wait for the door to open and then I would reach out and touch the person's neck. If I felt the furry collar, I would know it was Susan—and I would get her back for scaring me like this. If I didn't feel the furry collar . . . well, then there was nothing I could do.

The shuffling footsteps had reached the second flight of stairs. I forced my own feet to take the steps to get near the door of the room. I felt the skin crawl on my back as the footsteps reached the top step and moved down the hallway. I braced myself. The door creaked slightly as it swung open. I reached my arms out and hoped.

My fingers closed around the thick fur of Susan's collar. My body drained with relief. I moved my hands up to touch Susan's face. I was so happy; I no longer wanted to scare her. But as my fingers moved up from the furry collar, there was nothing.

Only the bloody stump where Susan's head had been.

THE BLACK
VELVET RIBBON

There was one room in the house that the old man always kept locked. Things had not changed in that room for years. A soft layer of dust had settled on the furniture and on the thing that lay on the floor, beside the bed. . . .

The old man had been a bachelor most of his life. When he was 40 years old, he had met her—the girl with the black velvet ribbon. She was beautiful in a strange, mysterious way. Her hair and her deep, bottomless eyes were as black as the velvet ribbon around her neck. He planned to marry her before the next full moon rose in the autumn sky.

On their wedding day, he watched her walk toward him up the long aisle. She was dressed in a white gown, a white veil, and carried a bouquet of white flowers. Even her face was ivory white. But below it, around the ivory neck, was the black velvet ribbon. He remembered staring at that ribbon as the strains of the wedding march brought his bride nearer to him. He remembered the curious and shocked looks on the faces of the wedding guests. But then his eyes met hers, and he was drowning in their bottomless darkness.

He didn't think of the velvet ribbon during the rest of his wedding day. It was a joyous time, and if people thought his wife a bit strange, they kept it to themselves. That night, when they were alone, he saw that the ribbon was still there, still circling her lovely neck.

"Don't you ever take that ribbon from around your neck?" he asked, hoping his question was a needless one.

"You'll be sorry if I do," his wife answered, "so I won't."

Her answer disturbed him, but he did not question her further. There was plenty of time for her to change her ways.

Their life together fell into a pleasant pattern. They were happy, as most newly married couples are. He found her to be a perfect wife . . . well, nearly perfect. Although she had a great number of dresses and wore a different one every day, she never changed the black velvet ribbon. This ribbon began to be the test of their marriage. When he looked at her, his eyes would inevitably fall to her neck. When he kissed her, he could feel the ribbon tightening around his own throat.

"Won't you please take that ribbon from around your neck?" he asked her time and time again.

"You'll be sorry if I do, so I won't." This was always her answer. At first it teased him. Then it began to grate on his nerves. Now it was beginning to infuriate him.

"You'll be sorry if I do."

"You'll be sorry if I do."

One day he tried to pull the ribbon off after she had repeated her answer, like a mechanical doll. It wouldn't come loose from her neck. He realized then, for the first time, that the ribbon had no beginning and no end. It circled her neck like a band of steel. He had drawn back from her in disgust that day. Things weren't the same with them after that.

At the breakfast table, the black ribbon seemed to mock him as he drank his suddenly bitter coffee. In the afternoon, outside, the ribbon made a funeral out of the sunlight. But it was at night that the ribbon bothered him most. He knew he could live with it no longer.

"Either take that ribbon off, or I will," he said on a night to his wife of only four weeks.

"You'll be sorry if I do, so I won't." She smiled at him, and then fell off to sleep.

But he did not sleep. He lay there, staring at the hated ribbon. He had meant what he said. If she would not take off the ribbon, he would.

As she lay sleeping and unsuspecting, he crept out of bed and over to her sewing box. He had seen a small, sharp scissors she kept there. It was thin enough, he knew, to slip between the velvet ribbon and her soft neck. Gripping the scissors in his trembling hands, he walked softly back to the bed. He came up to where she lay and stood over her. Her head was thrown back on the pillow, and her throat with the black velvet ribbon around it rose ever so slightly with her breathing.

He bent down, and with one swift movement, he forced the thin blade of the scissors under the ribbon. Then, with a quick, triumphant snip, he severed the ribbon that had come between them.

The black velvet ribbon fell away from his wife's neck . . . her head rolled off the bed and onto the floor. . . . She was muttering, "You'll be sorry, you'll be sorry . . ."

THE BOARDER

The boy lay quietly in the dark. He was listening. Next door, the boarder was making the sounds of preparing for bed. The boy could hear him brush his teeth, gargle, and then splash water onto his face. The sounds made the boy grit his teeth. He hated the boarder.

The two of them shared the upstairs floor of the house. It was a small house in the poor area of town. The boy's parents had taken the boarder in to add his rent to their meager income. Before, the boy had had the upstairs to himself. The extra bedroom had been his playroom. Now the boy was kept to his own small space.

In the next room, the boarder was getting his bed ready for the night. The boy heard him plump the pillows. Then he heard the creak of the old bedsprings as the boarder lay down. The boy wondered if the boarder knew how well he could be heard, how much the boy

9

knew about every move he made. The sound of the light switch being flicked off came through the thin walls. Now, the boy knew, the boarder was lying in the dark, too. Listening for him.

It was a waiting game. The boy knew the boarder would be going out tonight. For the last month, he had known about the Friday-night journeys. This night, the boy planned to follow the boarder to wherever it was that he went.

The boy lay perfectly still in his bed. He had learned how to be very quiet. It bothered him to think that the boarder could hear him as he could hear the boarder. So he had begun to walk softly and creep slowly into bed and to do everything quietly — like a cat. The boarder didn't know how much the boy could hear from his room.

But no sound came from the boarder's room now, except the muffled sound of snoring. The boy hated that snoring, just as he hated everything about the boarder. He hated his snickering laugh and the way the boarder looked at his mother at the breakfast table. He despised his chores of shining the boarder's shoes and going on errands for him. Most of all, he hated the boarder's money, which his parents needed so much.

The money was the reason the boy lay awake in bed. No one knew how the boarder got his money. No one knew how he spent his days away from the house. No one asked questions because the rent money was always there, fully paid and in advance. The boy lay in the dark and struggled to keep his eyes open. Tonight he was going to follow the boarder and find out his secret.

The seconds of time ticked by in the boy's mind as he lay waiting. He knew the boarder would pretend to sleep like this at first. But the time was drawing near now for him to make his move. The boy waited in silent darkness.

Then, from the next room, came the slow creaking of springs. The boy raised his head to hear better. The springs creaked again as the boarder's weight crushed against them. Then, they were quiet. Now the boy knew that the boarder was preparing for his journey. He would be slipping into his clothes in the dark, pulling on his rubber-soled shoes.

The boy slipped out of bed and reached for his own clothes. He didn't make a sound as he dressed himself and put on his sneakers. He tiptoed over to the window in his room and pressed himself against the wall. He was ready.

The window in the boarder's room slid open with a slight scratching noise of wood against wood. The boy stared sideways out his window. He watched as two legs quietly and carefully picked their way across the small balcony outside the window.

The legs disappeared. For a few seconds, the boy heard no sound. Then there was a dull thud on the ceiling above him. The boarder had gotten up onto the roof.

Moving quietly like the boarder, the boy slid open his window. He swung his body over the sill and onto the small balcony. He knew he was taking a chance of the boarder seeing him. But he knew if he waited too long, the boarder might be out of sight.

The boy climbed the drainage pipe up to the roof as the boarder had done before him. He slowly raised his eyes to the level of the roof. Standing twenty feet away and staring across the roof tops, was the boarder.

The boy could see the eager expression on his face. He could also see the shiny hook hanging from his belt and the coil of thick rope hung over his shoulder.

The boy lowered his head below the roof top. Then he heard the boarder move across the roof. He peeked out again, over the roof. The boarder had jumped from their house to the next one. The roofs were only four feet apart because the houses were built so close together in this neighborhood. The boy saw the boarder walk across that roof and then jump to the next house.

It was a dark night. The moon was hidden by clouds. The boy hoisted himself onto the roof. He crept over to the chimney. Three houses away, he could see the boarder walking steadily east.

He knew he had to follow the boarder fast enough to keep up with him, but slowly enough not to be seen. The boy came to the space between his house and the next one. The cement walkway between the two houses stared up at him from forty feet below. He felt sick for a moment. Then he leapt across to the next roof.

As he landed, he saw the boarder turn around from three houses away. The boy flattened himself against the tar roof. He watched as the boarder paused, searching the darkness for the source of the sound he had heard. But the boarder couldn't see the boy's body pressed up against the roof. He went on, jumping to the next roof to the east.

The boy made his next jump more quietly. The boarder didn't turn around. It became like a game of leap frog between them. The boarder jumping; then the boy jumping, three houses behind him. The boy learned not to look down at the black, gaping spaces between the roofs. His face, too, took on an expression of eager excitement.

Ahead, the boy could see that they were coming to the end of the block of small houses. As the boarder came to the last house, he turned left and began to cross the roofs going north. The boy knew that these roofs were no longer set apart. They were the roofs of the stores on Main Street, which were built right beside one another.

The boy ran softly to a chimney and crouched behind it, resting. The boarder, too, had stopped. He seemed to be counting the roofs of the connected buildings with his outstretched hand. Then he moved on down the roofs, walking confidently now. The boy followed slowly, bent down low. The roofs were flatter here than they had been on the houses. He followed behind the line of chimneys that stretched out in a row across the roofs.

Suddenly, deliberately, the boarder stopped in front of one of the chimneys. The boy jerked his body to a halt and darted behind the closest chimney. When he peeked around it, he saw the boarder shrugging the heavy coil of rope off his shoulder. He picked up the end of the rope and began to wind the coil around the chimney. The boy watched as he worked to make a strong knot in the rope. Then the boarder picked up the rest of the coil of rope and dropped it down the chimney. After a few seconds, a dull thud came from inside the bricks.

The boy sat behind the chimney, watching intently. His mind was in a fever. Now he knew the boarder's secret.

The metal hook from the boarder's belt flashed in the dull moonlight. The boy watched the boarder fasten the hook onto the chimney ledge. Then, as the moon shone brightly from an opening in the cloudly sky, the boy could see the boarder slowly descending into the chimney. As the boarder's head disappeared, the boy moved quickly across the roofs. He came up to the chimney tied round with the boarder's rope. He sat down and listened.

The boarder's grunts came up the chimney as he lowered himself down the rope. The boy knew what the boarder planned to do. He was looking for an old open fireplace. He could enter a store, rob it, and return up the chimney by rope. There would be no chance of a fire burning on such a hot summer's night.

The boarder's grunts disgusted the boy. Now that he knew the boarder's secret, he hated him even more. He eyed the rope twisted around the chimney. The knot was directly in front of him.

The boy touched the knot. It wasn't a very good one. He began to undo the loose end, thinking how stupid the boarder was. He began to pick at the knot more, thinking of how the boarder looked at his mother. He began to tug the loose end of the rope through the final tie, thinking of how the boarder's room used to be his. The knot came undone and the rope started to slip around the chimney. Then, suddenly, it disappeared down through the top. Seconds later, the boy heard a startled cry come from the chimney, followed by a dull thud.

The boy sat crouched near the roof. He knew the boarder had fallen. It sounded as though he had landed on the sealed bottom of the chimney. The boy wondered if the boarder was dead.

But then he heard the boarder's voice, grunting with effort. He listened to the voice for a long time as the boarder desperately tried to climb back up the chimney. He listened until the boarder's voice took on the mad sound of panic.

Then he ran away. He ran across the store roofs, across the house roofs, jumping from one to another. He reached the roof of his own house and swung himself down the pipe onto the small balcony. Quietly, he slipped through the window and shut it. In the still darkness he dropped his clothes on the floor and stole into bed.

It was six years later. Three more boarders had come and gone. The boy was eighteen now and he rented the extra upstairs room himself. His parents never asked him where he got the money. He joked that he did night work.

One morning, he went down to breakfast, as usual. His mother had his food and his newspaper waiting for him on the table. She gave him all the attention now that she used to give the boarders. As he sipped his coffee, he picked up the morning paper. He leafed through it, reading the headlines. Then, a small article caught his eye.

The boy read it, slowly. And the whole time, his fingers worked unconsciously . . . going through the motions of untying a knot.

BODY FOUND IN CHIMNEY

Sept. 17—Yesterday workmen discovered the remains of a body in an old sealed-off chimney. A coroner on the scene said that the person had been dead for at least five years. Authorities suspect that a cat-burglar, trying to rob a jewelry store in the building, had become stuck in the chimney. Because of the advanced deterioration of the body, no identification could be made. The only possessions found with the body were a steel hook and an old rope.

THE
TEN CLAWS

Long ago, a small village was plagued by a monster. The monster had never been seen nor heard; it never left tracks or evidence. The only proof of its existence was its victims.

The victims were always killed in the same way—ten jagged holes would be found in their necks. At first, the monster attacked only small animals. A farmer woke one morning to find that three of his sheep had bled to death. Then, three pet dogs in the village were found dead with the same strange claw marks in their necks.

Rumors circulated in the village. Everyone heard about the animals. But no one could give a logical explanation for what had killed them. Next, a young calf was found dead. It had bled to death, too, its jugular vein punctured by the ten mysterious holes. After this, men began to arm themselves. Shotguns were set beside beds at night. Animals were kept locked in the barns.

Throughout the village, a rash of hysteria broke loose. People put forth all kinds of wild speculation. Neighbors eyed each other with suspicion.

Then it happened — what everyone had really feared. The monster attacked a human, Elmer Riley, the town drunk. Elmer was found dead one morning, with the ten claw holes in his neck. He had died just like the sheep and the dogs and the calf: He had bled to death. Not many people in the town really cared that Elmer was dead. But it scared them to know that the monster had an appetite for humans as well. Anyone could be its prey.

The men in the village banded together to form a vigilante group. They didn't know what they were fighting, which made things even worse. Robert and John Harmon, two brothers, were appointed head of the vigilante committee. They lived on the outskirts of the village, near the forest where most people thought the monster lived. The two brothers knew how the monster attacked. It had been their calf that was killed.

After the first meeting of the vigilante committee, Robert and John Harmon went home to discuss their plans. They sat around the oak table in the kitchen with their father. Their old grandmother sat by the fireplace on a low chair, her black shawl wrapped around her.

"We must begin the watch tonight," Robert

said in a low voice. "The other men are afraid to act now, but I think tonight is the time to be on guard."

"You're right," his brother agreed. "The thing — whatever it is — strikes every five days. It was five nights ago that Elmer Riley was killed."

"You boys sound brave," their father interrupted," but remember what you are dealing with. The thing seems to attack without warning. In the killings so far, there were no signs of struggle. How will you know what to watch for?"

The father paused and looked over to his old mother sitting by the fireplace. "They should be careful, shouldn't they, Granny."

The old woman looked up at her son. She shuddered for a moment, and then fell silent again. The three men went back to their conversation. They hadn't really expected to get an answer from her. Her mind had been foggy for years.

Robert began to outline his plan to his father. "John and I will both take our guns to the outskirts of the forest tonight. We'll set ourselves up on the path between the forest and the village. If the monster comes out tonight, it will have to pass by either of us."

"And what protection will you have?" the father asked worriedly.

"Each other," Robert answered. "We'll stay

within shouting distance of each other. And we'll keep our backs to the village so that we face the forest . . . and the monster."

"Someone has to do it," John said to his father. "We don't know who the next victim will be. We can't just sit back and let the monster kill us off, one by one."

Their father stood up from the table and walked around the room once. Then he shook each of their hands. "Come back to me alive," he said, his voice choking.

The two sons picked up their rifles from the floor. Robert pulled a long, sharp machete from off the wall.

As they left the room, both of them walked over to their old grandmother and kissed her good-bye.

Outside, the night was nearly pitch black. A thin sliver of a moon hung low in the western sky. They walked east, toward the forest. As they drew near to where they had planned to station themselves, John whispered, "I wonder what it looks like?"

"I've been thinking," Robert said, "that it could be a bird. A giant bird that swoops down on you and digs its claws into your neck."

They both looked up into the night sky. Clouds had shrouded the thin moon. It would be hard to see a dark shadow descending through the sky.

"I thought it might tunnel under the

ground, like a huge weasel," John said softly. "Then it comes out and attacks you from behind."

Both brothers felt the skin crawl on the backs of their necks. Slowly, they both turned and looked behind them.

For several minutes, they stood together like that in the dark, paralyzed by their own horrible thoughts.

"We must take our places," Robert said finally. "But, remember, stay within shouting distance."

The two brothers moved off in opposite directions. They had agreed that each would take twenty long paces and then stop.

Standing in the dark, Robert carefully cocked his gun. Then he took the machete and stuck it in the soft ground by his feet. He waited.

Forty paces away, John fumbled nervously with his gun. He felt his hands shaking. Could he use the gun if he had to? He wished he could see Robert, but his brother was obscured by the dark shadows of bushes and trees.

John turned around to look toward the village. He wished he were safe inside the house. Then he heard the crackling of a twig in back of him. He spun around to face the forest. But he saw nothing and heard no more.

John relaxed. He set the butt of his gun down in the ground and leaned against it. He started to feel drowsy.

Then, he felt the ten claws, digging into his neck.

A terrified scream echoed through the forest to Robert. He grabbed his gun and machete and followed the awful screams to his brother. He drew near, but couldn't see anything in the dark night.

But then he heard John's voice, choking and desperate. "Quick, swing the machete behind where you hear my voice . . . Hurry."

Robert threw down his gun and grasped the machete in both hands. He swung it above his head and let it fall. It made a hacking sound before it hit the ground.

John had been groaning the whole time, but now he stopped. For an instant, Robert thought he had killed his brother. But then John started to babble incoherently.

Robert thought he heard something moving back away from them. It sounded like a giant rat scuttling over the dead leaves. But he could not see it. He fell down on the ground by his brother's body.

Moaning again, John took his brother's hand and put it to his own neck. Robert shrunk back at what he felt. It was a hand, a withered hand with sharp, pointed claws. He had hacked it off the monster with his machete. And it was still stuck in John's neck.

Robert jerked the foul claws from his brother's neck. Then he bound the ten bloody holes with his handkerchief. He carried his brother back to the village, leaving the withered hand lying on the forest floor.

Their father met them at the door, weeping with fear. He had heard John's terrified screams in the forest. Now he wept with happiness to see that both his sons were alive yet.

They laid John out on a couch and washed out the claw marks in his neck. They could see that a few seconds more and the claws would have killed him. As he bandaged his brother's neck, Robert thought about the monster. He hoped it was in the forest now, dying a slow death.

All this time, no one had noticed that the old woman was gone from her spot by the fireplace. And no one noticed when she came in through the back door and sat down there again. From her low seat, she looked over to Robert and John.

No one heard the hiss that came from her wrinkled mouth. And no one saw the bloody stump that she hid under her black shawl.

THE JIGSAW PUZZLE

It was on the top shelf of an old bookcase, covered with dust and barely visible. Lisa decided she had to find out what it was. Of all the things in the old junk shop, it aroused her curiosity most. She had looked through old books, prints, and postcards for hours. Nothing had caught her interest. Now the old box, high and out of reach, intrigued her.

She looked around for the old man who ran the store. But he had gone into the back room. She saw a stepladder across the room and brought it over to the bookcase. It shook on the uneven floorboards as she climbed to the top step.

Lisa patted her hand along the surface of the top shelf, trying to find the box. The dirt was thick and gritty on the board. Then she touched the box. It was made of cardboard. The cardboard was cold and soft from being in the damp room for such a long time. She lifted the box down slowly, trying to steady her balance on the stepladder.

As the side of the box reached her eye level, she could read the words:

500 PIECES

She sat the box down on top of the stepladder and climbed down a few steps. Then she blew away some of the dust that had accumulated on the lid. It billowed up around her with a musty, dead odor. But now she could make out a few more words on top of the box:

THE STRANGEST
JIGSAW PUZZLE
IN THE WORLD

There were other words underneath that, but they had been rubbed off the cardboard lid. The big picture on the cover had been curiously damaged. Lisa could make out areas of light and dark. It looked as though the scene might be in a room. But most of the picture had been scratched off the cardboard box, probably by a sharp instrument.

The mysterious nature of the jigsaw puzzle made it even more appealing to Lisa. She decided she would buy it. The lid was taped down securely; that probably meant that all the pieces would be there. As she carefully climbed down the stepladder, holding the box in both hands, Lisa smiled to herself. It was quite a find, just the sort of thing she had always hoped to discover while rummaging through secondhand stores.

Mr. Tuborg, the owner of the store, came out of the back room as she was walking up to his sales desk. He looked curiously at the box when Lisa set it down.

"And where did you find that?" he asked her.

Lisa pointed to where she had set up the stepladder. "It was on top of that bookcase. You could barely see it from the floor."

"Well, I've never seen it before, that's for sure," Mr. Tuborg said. "Can't imagine how you found it."

Lisa was more pleased than ever about her find. She felt as though the puzzle had been hiding up there, waiting for her to discover it. She paid Mr. Tuborg the twenty-five cents he asked for the puzzle and then wrapped it carefully in the newspapers he gave her to take it home in.

It was late on a Saturday afternoon. Lisa lived alone in a small room in an old apartment house. She had no plans for Saturday night. Now she decided to spend the whole evening working on the puzzle. She stopped at a delicatessen and bought some meat, bread, and cheese for sandwiches. She would eat while she put the puzzle together.

As soon as she had climbed the flight of

stairs to her room and put away the groceries, Lisa cleaned off the big table in the center of the room. She set the box down on it.

THE STRANGEST
JIGSAW PUZZLE
IN THE WORLD

Lisa read the words again. She wondered what they could mean. How strange could a jigsaw puzzle be?

The tape that held the lid down was still strong. Lisa got out a kitchen knife to slice through it. When she lifted the cover off the box, a musty smell came from inside. But the jigsaw pieces all looked in good condition. Lisa picked one up. The color was faded, but the picture was clear. She could see the shape of a finger in the piece. It looked like a woman's finger.

Lisa sat down and started to lay out the pieces, top side up, on the large table. As she took them from the box, she sorted out the flat-edged pieces from the inside pieces. Every so often, she would recognize something in one of the pieces. She saw some blonde hair, a window pane, and a small vase. There was a lot of wood texture in the pieces, plus what looked like wallpaper. Lisa noticed that the wallpaper in the puzzle looked a lot like the wallpaper in her own room. She wondered if her wallpaper was as old as the jigsaw puzzle. It would be an incredible coincidence, but it could be the same.

By the time Lisa had all the pieces laid out on the table, it was 6:30. She got up and made herself a sandwich. Already, her back was beginning to hurt a little from leaning over the table. But she couldn't stay away from the puzzle. She went back to the table and set her sandwich down beside her. It was always like that when she did jigsaws. Once she started, she couldn't stop until the puzzle was all put together.

She began to sort out the edge pieces according to their coloring. There were dark brown pieces, whitish pieces, the wallpaper pieces, and some pieces that seemed to be like glass—perhaps a window. As she slowly ate her sandwich, Lisa pieced together the border. When she was finished, she knew she had been right about the setting of the picture when she had first seen the puzzle. It was a room. One side of the border was wallpaper. Lisa decided to fill that in first. She was curious about its resemblance to her own wallpaper.

She gathered all the pieces together that had the blue and lilac flowered design. As she fit the pieces together, it became clear that the wallpaper in the puzzle was identical to the wallpaper in her room. Lisa glanced back and forth between the puzzle and her wall. It was an exact match.

By now it was 8:30. Lisa leaned back in her chair. Her back was stiff. She looked over at her window. The night was black outside. Lisa got up and walked over to the window. Suddenly, she felt uneasy, alone in the apartment. She pulled the white shade over the window.

She paced around the room once, trying to think of something else she might do than finish the puzzle. But nothing else interested her. She went back and sat down at the table.

Next she started to fill in the lower right-hand corner. There was a rug and then a chair. This part of the puzzle was very dark. Lisa noticed uneasily that the chair was the same shape as one sitting in the corner of her room. But the colors didn't seem exactly the same. Her chair was maroon. The one in the puzzle was in the shadows and seemed almost black.

Lisa continued to fill in the border toward the middle. There was more wallpaper to finish on top. The left-hand side did turn out to be a window. Through it, a half moon hung in a dark sky. But it was the bottom of the puzzle that began to bother Lisa. As the pieces fell into place, she saw a picture of a pair of legs, crossed underneath a table. They were the legs of a young woman. Lisa reached down and ran her hand along one of her legs. Suddenly, she had felt as though something was crawling up it, but it must have been her imagination.

She stared down at the puzzle. It was almost three quarters done. Only the middle remained. Lisa glanced at the lid to the puzzle box:

THE STRANGEST
JIGSAW . . .

She shuddered.

Lisa leaned back in her chair again. Her back ached. Her neck muscle were tense and strained. She thought about quitting the puzzle. It scared her now.

She stood up and stretched. Then she looked down at the puzzle on the table. It looked different from the higher angle. Lisa was shocked by what she saw. Her body began to tremble all over.

It was unmistakable — the picture in the puzzle was of her own room. The window was placed correctly in relation to the table. The bookcase stood in its exact spot against the wall. Even the carved table legs were the same . . .

Lisa raised her hand to knock the pieces of the puzzle apart. She didn't want to finish the strangest jigsaw puzzle in the world; she didn't want to find out what the hole in the middle of the puzzle might turn out to be.

But then she lowered her hand. Perhaps it was worse not to know. Perhaps it was worse to wait and wonder.

Lisa sank back down into the chair at the table. She fought off the fear that crept into the sore muscles of her back. Deliberately, piece by piece, she began to fill in the hole in the puzzle. She put together a picture of a table, on which lay a jigsaw puzzle. This puzzle inside the puzzle was finished. But Lisa couldn't make out what it showed. She pieced together the young woman who was sitting at the table—the young woman who was herself. As she filled in the picture, her own body slowly filled with horror and dread. It was all there in the picture . . . the vase filled with blue cornflowers, her red cardigan sweater, the wild look of fear in her own face.

The jigsaw puzzle lay before her—finished except for two adjoining pieces. They were dark pieces, ones she hadn't been able to fit into the area of the window. Lisa looked behind her. The white blind was drawn over her window. With relief, she realized that the puzzle picture was not exactly like her room. It showed the black night behind the window pane and a moon shining in the sky.

With trembling hands, Lisa reached for the second to last piece. She dropped it into one of the empty space. It seemed to be half a face, but not a human face. She reached for the last piece. She pressed it into the small hole left in the picture.

The face was complete—the face in the window. It was more horrible than anything she had ever seen, or dreamed. Lisa looked at the picture of herself in the puzzle and then back to that face.

Then she whirled around. The blind was no longer over her window. The night showed black through the window pane. A half moon hung low in the sky.

Lisa screamed . . . the face . . . it was there, too.

THE FACE

It was during the California Gold Rush of 1849. Three men were holed up in a small cabin for the night. They sat around the jumping flames of the fire and warmed themselves. Outside, the wind whistled and moaned through the canyon. Every so often, a coyote howled.

The three men were old friends. They had shared the hopes and disappointments of gold prospecting. This was their last night out in the hills. The next day, they planned on heading to San Francisco to find work. All of them were broke.

"Blasted coyotes," Billy said.

"They're hungry tonight. We're lucky we found this place," Jeremiah said slowly.

Another coyote howled above the sound of the wind. This one was closer. The three men looked at each other nervously.

"I still don't like moving into deserted cabins like this," the third man, named Dusty, complained. "You don't know why people left." He paused for a minute. "And they don't leave without a reason."

"You can go out and sleep with the coyotes if you want, Dusty," Jeremiah said as he rolled out his sleeping bag.

The fire was beginning to burn lower. The other two men rolled out their bags and settled down for the night. All was silent inside the cabin. Outside, the coyotes and the wind kept up their eerie symphony.

Jeremiah woke from his deep sleep with a start. He looked around, trying to remember where he was. The cabin, yes, the cabin . . . he thought drowsily. But what woke him? He lay his head back down and shut his eyes. Then he heard it . . . the breathing. It was fast, excited breathing, coming in short gasps. He looked over to the fireplace where Billy was sprawled out, asleep.

Jeremiah's blood froze at what he saw. A face . . . nothing but the hideous face of an old woman . . . was hovering over Billy's body. The short gasps of breathing were coming from this hag's face. Jeremiah could see the lips opening and closing with the breathing.

"Billy," he screamed.

Billy shuddered in his sleep. Then he raised himself to his elbows and slowly opened his eyes. His face was only two inches from the face of the hag. Jeremiah watched as his eyes widened in horror as he looked at it. The hag's face was old and wrinkled. The skin was blistered by the sun and disease. Hair stood out on the head like twisting snakes. The eyes were full of hate.

Jeremiah could hear its panting breath come faster. Billy parted his lips in a scream. Then, the hag breathed a long, deep breath into his lungs. As Billy's body slumped back, the face disappeared.

"My god," Jeremiah said softly. He didn't believe in ghosts. And his mind couldn't make any sense of what he had just seen. But that didn't make any difference now. He kicked Dusty with his foot to wake him up. Then he ran over to Billy's body. Billy was dead.

"We gotta get out of here, Dusty," Jeremiah yelled. "Billy's dead . . . there was a face . . . an old hag's face. . . . I don't know, a ghost or something . . ."

Dusty was lying on his sleeping bag, eyeing Jeremiah suspiciously. "You cracked up, Jeremiah?" he asked.

But Dusty didn't say any more. Because he found out what Jeremiah meant. The face materialized out of the air in front of him. Once again, the cabin was filled with the sound of its breathing.

Dusty's face worked itself into an expression of horror.

"Keep your mouth shut, Dusty," Jeremiah screamed in warning.

But it was too late. Dusty's mouth opened wide in a scream. The hag's face breathed death into his body through its withered lips. Then it disappeared.

Jeremiah backed against the cabin wall. He looked down at his two dead friends.

A coyote pierced the silence with its hungry howl.

Jeremiah ran for the door. A foot away from escape, the hag's face appeared before him. Jeremiah's legs stiffened with fright. His hand froze on the door latch.

The old woman's eyes were looking into his eyes. He could see the pattern of wrinkles and scars on her face. He could feel her panting breath against his face. Jeremiah felt himself choking. His breath seemed stuck in his lungs. The face was coming nearer and nearer. He struggled to keep his mouth shut. He thought of Billy and Dusty.

He jerked aside the door latch and threw the cabin door open, watching as the door swung right through the hag's face. She disappeared once again. Jeremiah grabbed the rifle by the door and ran down into the canyon. He ran until he felt his lungs would burst. His own hard breathing haunted him. It sounded like the breathing of the hag, following him. He kept running until the night broke into daylight.

Finally, he threw himself down, exhausted, on a flat rock. For the first time since his escape from the cabin, he began to gather his distracted thoughts. Billy and Dusty were dead. Something had killed them. Jeremiah could still see the hag's hideous face in his mind. What was she? he wondered. The mad ghost of a prospector's wife, seeking revenge? An evil spirit left by the Indians who had been forced out of these mountains by the gold rush? Or was it the face that death wore? And now that she had shown herself to him, was there any escape?

Suddenly, Jeremiah realized how horrible his situation was. Someone was sure to find Billy's and Dusty's dead bodies. And nobody would believe his story about the hag's face. Of course not. He would be accused of the murders. People would say he had killed his partners for gold. And there would be no way he could explain it.

For a moment, Jeremiah thought he might go crazy. Then, he realized there was only one way out for him. He had to get out of the mountains, fast, before someone found Billy's and Dusty's bodies.

Far in the distance, he saw the dusty trail of a stagecoach. It was coming his way up the mountain. That was the answer, he decided. He would ride the stagecoach out of the territory. Jumping to his feet, Jeremiah ran down the canyon to the stagecoach road below. He had a little time to catch his breath before he flagged down the stagecoach driver.

"Get in, there's plenty room," the driver shouted at him.

As Jeremiah climbed into the coach, he saw that there was only one other passenger — a woman. He settled back into his seat and looked across at her. She was young and beautiful. He smiled to himself as he thought of his luck. He had escaped the horrible death-breathing hag. And now he was sitting across from this charming girl.

The young woman saw him looking at her. She smiled shyly back at Jeremiah. The stage-coach rocked slowly from side to side. Jeremiah's tense body began to relax. Everything will work out all right, he thought to himself as he drifted off into a contented sleep.

He woke suddenly with a start. His heart was pounding wildly. For a moment, he couldn't remember where he was. The stage-coach, yes, the stagecoach . . . he thought drowsily. But what had awakened him?

Then he heard it . . . the breathing. It was fast, excited breathing, coming in short gasps. Jeremiah looked up. The young woman was staring at him. He saw her lovely lips opening and closing with her breathing.

Jeremiah's eyes took on a wild look. He thought of Billy and Dusty. The breathing seemed to get louder; it seemed to pound in his ears. He crouched into the corner of the stagecoach. Desperately, he looked out of the window. The coach was going around a hairpin curve. Below, a cliff fell sharply to the deep canyon below.

He looked over at the woman again. She was still staring at him. Her breath was coming louder still. The whole stagecoach seemed filled by it.

"No," Jeremiah moaned softly.

"Is there something wrong?" the young woman asked as she got up from her seat and then sat down beside Jeremiah.

Jeremiah shrank back against the stagecoach door. He watched as the woman's face came closer to him. She was lifting her hand to his forehead. He could feel her breathing against his face.

"No . . ." Jeremiah screamed as he turned the latch on the door and jumped out of the stagecoach. His scream echoed up from the canyon as his body tumbled down the steep cliff.

Then, the young woman heard no more. She sat sobbing in the stagecoach, terrified with fright. It was her first trip West. And that man who had just leaped to his death. . . . she had never seen him before.

THE MIRROR

Hugo Hoogen lived alone. He had no family, no real friends, not even a pet. Monday through Friday he went to work at his office. Hugo was an accountant. Every day he added columns of numbers. Once every two weeks he made out the paychecks for his company. That was the closest he ever came to the other employees—typing their names on a paycheck.

Hugo spent the weekends alone. On Saturdays he watched television, and he carefully read through every piece of junk mail he had received during the week. Hugo always answered the ads for free information. On Sundays he read the newspaper and took a walk. He didn't mind living such a solitary life. He didn't like people, really. But sometimes, Hugo could tell when he had been alone too long. Sometimes, when he had to talk to someone, his voice sounded like a stranger's. When that happened, he made a point of eating out in a restaurant. He would ask the waitress questions and listen to what other people were saying. That usually got him back to normal.

One Monday morning, Hugo woke up at exactly 7:30, as he did every other morning. It had been a three-day weekend because of a holiday on Friday. Hugo had not left his apartment for three days. The weather had been too bad to take a walk on Sunday. So he had stayed in and watched television and read the papers.

Hugo groaned and stumbled out of bed. His head felt groggy this morning. He went into the bathroom and turned on the cold water. Then he splashed his face with the water to try and clear his head. But he still felt strange.

After he had dried his face, Hugo looked in the mirror. He always did that in the morning. Hugo looked in the mirror for a long time this morning. He didn't seem to be thinking straight, and what he saw in the mirror didn't make sense. He stared straight into the reflection of his eyes. Then he looked at his nose, his mouth, his forehead. The more he looked at himself, the more it seemed that he was looking at the face of a stranger. That's not me, he thought to himself. That can't be me. But as he moved his face up and down, the reflection also moved up and down.

Hugo shut his eyes and shook his head back

and forth. Then he looked in the mirror again. The stranger's face hadn't gone away. It was staring right back at him.

"My God," said Hugo. He put his hands to his face. It felt the same. Suddenly he needed to know that he was still himself. He ran to his closet. His clothes were all neatly hung in rows, arranged according to color. He pulled open a dresser drawer. His wallet was there, and the driver's license had his name on it. Hugo sighed with relief.

Then he looked up at the mirror over the dresser. The stranger was looking back at him.

"That isn't me," Hugo said in a trembling voice. "I don't look like that."

He dressed himself in one of his oldest suits, one that he had worn hundreds of times. It made him feel secure.

Then he went into the kitchen, put on some coffee, and poured himself a bowl of cereal. As he picked up the big cereal spoon, he saw the stranger's distorted face, staring at him upside down. "I don't look like that," Hugo repeated.

Suddenly he thought of a way to prove it. A picture, he thought; there must be a picture of me. But he couldn't think of any. No one had ever taken a picture of him that he could remember. He began to shake inside. Wasn't there any way to prove that he wasn't the stranger he saw reflected in mirrors?

By now it was 8:15. He would have to be at his desk in forty-five minutes. Hugo didn't know what to do. He couldn't go into his office looking like a stranger. But he couldn't stay home, either. It was the fifteenth of the month. The employees were supposed to get their checks today.

Hugo got ready to go to the office. He avoided looking in any mirrors. As he locked the door to his apartment, his neighbor, Mrs. Reynolds, passed him on the street.

"Good morning, Mr. Hoogen," she said.

Hugo returned her greeting. Then he realized what it meant. He looked like his old self to her. He almost went back into the apartment to look in a mirror. But then he remembered that there was a mirror at the front of the bus he took to his office.

He walked to the bus stop and waited, humming a song. He felt better now. The bus pulled up and Hugo walked on. As he gave the driver his money, he stooped to look into the mirror. To his horror, the stranger stared back, with an eager grin on his face.

Hugo slumped down into a seat. He rode all the way to his office with his eyes shut. There was a window by his seat, and every time he looked at it, the reflection of the stranger's face was there.

At 9:00, Hugo was in his office and at his desk. He sat there, waiting for someone to notice. But no one did. The women who worked in the accounts department with him acted perfectly normal. They paid no more attention to him than they usually did.

Hugo felt as though he were going mad. Four times during the day he went to the rest-room to check. The mirror always confirmed his fears. He looked like a total stranger. And no one had even noticed!

Hugo went home that night and went directly to bed. He hid in his darkened bedroom until sleep put his exhausted mind to rest.

When he woke the next morning he was afraid to look in the mirror. He avoided it. But he had to shave if he went to work. It was hard shaving the stranger's face; his hands were shaking.

It went like that Tuesday morning and Wednesday morning and Thursday morning.

Friday morning, Hugo woke up at 7:15 and lay in bed for a very long time. He didn't want to get up. He felt as though he couldn't go on, living with that stranger's face. He stayed in his bedroom for an hour.

Finally, the fear of being alone with the face all day forced him out of bed. He decided he would go to work, even though he was late. He went into the bathroom and began to shave automatically. Then he dropped his razor. It was his old face, his own face, back in the mirror again.

Hugo felt all over his face. It was really him. This was how he looked. He let out a crazy laugh. The stranger had gone, disappeared, and he was himself again.

Hugo finished shaving, dressed, and rushed out of the house without having breakfast. He was eager to go to work now, eager to have people see him.

As he was locking his front door, Mrs. Reynolds passed by on the street. She looked at him suspiciously and didn't say good morning. But Hugo was too happy to notice she was acting strangely.

He sprang up the steps into the bus and handed the driver his money. Stooping down, he saw his own face smiling back at him in the driver's mirror.

On the ride into the office, he would turn to the window every few minutes. He wanted constant reassurance that his face would be there in the reflection. It always was.

At 9:30, Hugo pushed open the door to the accounts department. The receptionist was calling to him from her desk in the hallway. But he didn't pay attention. He wanted to get to his desk. He was late.

Hugo strode across the room to his desk, which sat in a corner. He put his briefcase on the desk and sat down in his chair. He noticed that the constant sound of typing in the room had stopped. There was no sound at all, as a matter of fact.

Hugo smiled as he saw Miss Rose, the head clerk, walking toward his desk.

"Yes, Miss Rose," he said.

Miss Rose stopped a few feet from his desk. "Who are you?" she asked.

Hugo laughed at her joke. Miss Rose was being very friendly today.

"Why are you sitting in Mr. Hoogen's desk?" Miss Rose demanded.

Hugo stopped laughing. He looked into Miss Rose's eyes. The truth crept like a sinister madman into his mind. Miss Rose was looking at a total stranger. He could see that she didn't recognize him. Hugo gripped both sides of his desk.

"Who are you?" Miss Rose repeated.

But Hugo Hoogen didn't answer. His mind was too busy, making its strange spiraling descent . . . into total madness.

THE
EGYPTIAN
COFFIN

The night guard walked into the Egyptian section of the British museum. He gave a low whistle.

"A lot of weird stuff in here," he thought to himself.

It was the guard's first night of duty in the Egyptian rooms. He had been assigned to the Viking rooms of the museum for several months before this.

He plopped his fat body down on a hard bench by the wall. His bloodshot eyes surveyed the room. There were huge stone sculptures of lions with the heads of men, and wall paintings filled with strange symbols; there were jars, clothing, utensils and — this interested him most — mummies and coffins.

"I should have myself a good time in here," he muttered, and then he let out a cackling laugh.

The guard had had a good time in the Viking section of the museum, also. That was the reason for his transfer to the Egyptian wing. No one had been able to prove he had done it, of course. But he knew he was suspected. It was worth it, though. He had enjoyed scratching that word into the old Viking stone . . . and putting the cigarette butt into the mouth of the fake Viking warrior. . . . There were other things he had done, too, things they hadn't even caught yet.

He hated museums, always had, ever since his mother had dragged him through them as a child. And he didn't like being a night guard in this museum. But what else could he do? It was the only job he could find. Anyway, he made sure he didn't get bored.

The guard heaved his heavy body off the bench and began making a slow circuit around the long room. After a few steps, he stopped in front of a huge wall painting. It was filled with weird symbols and pictures of people with animal heads. A woman with the head of a bird, a man with the head of a cow; another man had the head of a fox. There was also a bird with the head of a man and a monstrous thing with the head of an alligator.

"Rubbish," the guard muttered. But he

stooped to see the title of the picture on the wall plaque.

"The Scale of Judgement" it read. Underneath the title were these words:

"The Egyptians thought that when a man died, his soul went before judges, all seated in a great hall. The judges wanted a report on the way he had behaved while on earth. Then the man's heart was weighed on a scale against a feather, the symbol of truth and justice. This was to find out if the man had spoken the truth to the judges. If he had lied, he was immediately eaten by a monster with a crocodile head."

The guard finished reading the plaque on the wall. Then he looked at the picture again. The scale was there, a heart on one side and a feather on the other. And the monster with the crocodile head was waiting, beside the scale.

The guard took a few steps backwards from the wall painting, but he didn't take his eyes off the crocodile. It fascinated him.

"Does it scare you?"

The voice made every muscle in the guard's body jump. He swung his fat body around to face the speaker.

It was the assistant curator of the museum, smiling.

"I didn't mean to scare you," the curator said in a slow, measured voice. "I wanted to know if the painting scared you."

The guard was embarrassed now. His embarrassment quickly turned to anger.

"That old junk doesn't scare me," he said. "What did you mean, sneaking up on me like that?" The guard glared down at the short curator.

"I didn't sneak up on you," the curator answered in his slow speech. "On the contrary, I walked quite normally. It's your job to be alert, after all."

The guard didn't reply. He was seething with anger.

"And furthermore," the curator went on, "this isn't junk. Our museum has one of the best collections of Egyptian artifacts in the world."

"Doesn't interest me," the guard said, walking away from the curator. "I think it's junk."

The curator's face turned red. "You watch yourself. We're onto your tricks, you know. If we weren't so short-staffed, I'd have you fired."

The guard turned around and stared at the curator with an insolent look on his face.

"You just watch yourself," the curator kept it up. "If you disturb anything in this room, you could be sorry. The Egyptians had great respect for their dead. They knew a lot about magic and curses. You had better not try any of your tricks in here."

The little curator continued his lecture until

he walked out of the room, slamming the door behind him.

The guard began his circuit of the room again. Now he had a surly scowl on his face. As he passed the Egyptian paintings and statues, he began to hate them more and more. The humans with animal heads seemed to threaten him with their beaks and claws and strange, passive faces.

"You had better watch yourself," the guard mimicked the curator's words. "They can have this job," he muttered.

The guard stopped to pull out a stick of chewing gum from his pocket. In front of him was a wooden coffin. A sign beside it said "Outer Coffin of Takheb, a Princess." It was in the shape of a human body. The coffin bottom lay flat on the floor. The decorated coffin lid stood upright at the foot of the bottom. As he began to chew his gum, the guard stared at the pictures on the decorated lid. The body of the lid was covered with feathers, human figures, snakes, and strange symbols. On the top of the lid, there was a face—the face of an Egyptian woman. She had large, almond-shaped, black eyes. The guard found himself staring into them.

"Oww!" The guard had bitten his tongue while chewing his gum. The pain snapped him back to reality. For a moment, he had become lost in that woman's eyes.

He put his fingers in his mouth and took out the gum. He looked around for a place to put it. Opposite the coffin was a mummy. Its sign said "Pedikhons, son of Takheb."

The guard looked at the mummy's human shape, wrapped in yellowing strips of cloth. He laughed under his breath. Then he stuck his piece of gum onto the back of the mummy's head. Now he laughed louder.

But, suddenly, he stopped. He felt as though someone was behind him, watching. He whirled around. But no one was there, just the coffin. The woman's eyes were staring at him, just as before.

The guard started to walk away from the coffin. But he found he couldn't take his eyes away from the woman's face. They seemed to be paralyzing his body. The first sickly feeling of fear crept into the guard's mind. He remembered the curator's words: "The Egyptians respected their dead. They had magic and curses." Then he remembered that the mummy was this woman's son.

The guard struggled to leave the spot where he stood. He swore at the coffin lid. He tried to reach out and knock it over. But he couldn't help himself. He seemed to be sinking deeper and deeper into the black eyes of the woman. Those eyes seemed to beckon him, to hypnotize him. They were like bottomless black pits set into the white, passive face of death.

The guard found himself being drawn forward, toward the coffin. His brain was slowing down, becoming sleepy. As he came within inches of the woman's eyes, suddenly they closed. Instantly, his own eyes went toward the coffin bottom. He saw that it was bigger than it had at first seemed, big enough for him to lie down in.

The guard was falling asleep. He let his body slip down into the soft, cushioned bottom of the coffin. He stretched himself out. With his hands by his side, his body fit perfectly.

Just before he fell asleep, the guard opened his eyes once more. He looked up at the inside of the coffin lid, which faced him at the bottom of his feet. He saw that the woman's face was painted on the inside of the lid, too. Her eyes were watching him. But these eyes were blacker yet, black with revenge.

The guard slipped off into strange dreams . . . just as the coffin lid fell neatly down over the coffin bottom. He lay in darkness, then—the air-tight, eternal darkness of an Egyptian coffin.

And, somewhere, the monster with a crocodile's head waited for him.

THE OLD PLANTATION

Jonas Ellerby turned his car into the plantation driveway at twilight. The long path from the road to the house was lined with giant cedar trees. Spanish moss drooped from their branches. The grass along the driveway had long ago turned to weeds. Now, already, the color of things was fading with the light. The trees were more like silhouettes, like shadows against the sky. Jonas felt the atmosphere of the place surround him. He was a Northerner. This landscape was new and strange to him.

The driveway took a sudden, sharp turn, and the house appeared. Jonas drew in his breath when he saw it. The house was not what he had expected. He had gotten his idea of Southern plantations from Hollywood movies.

Jonas stopped the car and turned off the engine. He stared at the great sweep of the house. Its long veranda stretched out underneath tall, white pillars. Window after window stared at him like curious eyes. In one, Jonas thought he saw a light go out. But then he decided it must have been a reflection.

Jonas looked up to the second story of the house. Something was wrong with it. The rooms sagged at a crazy angle to one side. The roof looked as though it had been blown on by too many storms. And the color of the house was not the blinding-bright whiteness of the plantations in the movies. It was a dull gray, an almost rotten gray color. It was a dying house. And Jonas had come to bury it.

Jonas represented the firm of Stanton and Stanton. The firm represented the estate of Mr. Whigover, the former owner of the house. The estate had gone into bankruptcy. Jonas had come to make plans to tear down the old house and sell off the land to a real estate dealer. Even though people had warned him that the house had a strange reputation, he had come this evening to spend the night in it.

Jonas got out of his car and slammed the car door shut. He decided he would explore the premises in the fading twilight. He followed the stone path up to the house and then walked up deteriorating steps onto the veranda. An old rocking chair sat there, moving slightly in the evening breeze. Jonas put the key he had been given into the front door lock. To his relief, the door opened.

As he stepped inside, Jonas was overwhelmed by the smell of dampness and decay. The air seemed steeped in the odor of age. He wondered how long it had been since another human had stepped foot inside this house.

He walked past the grand stairway which swept up to the second story, and entered a sitting room full of dusty, moldy furniture. His footsteps echoed on the bare floors as he went from room to room—the dining room, the ballroom, the study, the kitchen. Just as he was making his way back to the front door, Jonas passed a room he hadn't entered before. He opened the door and peeked in.

It was a small bedroom, sparsely decorated and neat. The sheets and pillowcases were no longer fresh but obviously clean. And this room didn't have the damp smell to it. Jonas stood and looked around the room for a moment. Then he smiled and went to get his luggage from the car.

By the time he had unpacked his things for the night and put them away, twilight had faded into night. Jonas knew the house had no electricity. But he saw that there was a partially burned candle on the nightstand by the bed.

As he fumbled with his matches in the darkness, he heard a chorus of crickets begin their shrill evening song. The candle blazed alight. That is when he first noticed the book. It was sitting on the nightstand, as if someone had laid it out for him. The title on the faded cover was *The Old Plantation*. Jonas decided he might read it later, when he turned in for the night.

Before that, though, Jonas thought he would go out onto the veranda one last time. As he walked out into the night air, he sensed a change in the atmosphere. He no longer felt just a few miles away from civilization. He felt isolated, and there seemed to be a different sense of time around the old plantation. The trees with their drooping Spanish moss closed in around the house. And there were no other sounds than the breathing of the trees in the dark and the piercing song of the crickets. Jonas moved nervously across the veranda. If he had known it would be like this, he wouldn't have come out.

He felt something alight on his face. Before he could brush it away, the mosquito had drawn his blood. Jonas felt his temple swelling with the bite. He decided to go back into the house.

Back in the bedroom, Jonas climbed into bed. He was shivering now. The candle on the nightstand was still burning. As he looked over at it, his eyes again fell upon the book and he picked it up. As he settled himself into bed, Jonas opened the pages to the first chapter. He read:

The story is about a young man, a Northerner, who comes to the South on business. One night, he drives his car up to an old Southern plantation. He decides to spend the night in the old house, even though he is all alone there . . .

Jonas slammed the book shut and laid it back down on the nightstand. He reached over and lit his pipe. His hands were shaking now as he struck another match. Then he lay back on the bed, taking long draws on his pipe. He could not get the strange coincidence of the book out of his mind. It made him nervous, but it made him curious, too. He reached over and picked up the book again.

In the story, the young man has just turned in for the night, after having gone out on the veranda for awhile. His face is still swollen from a mosquito bite he has gotten there. He scratches the bite.

Jonas caught himself scratching the bite on his own face. His hands began to tremble so badly that he couldn't hold the book still. He looked up at the ceiling of the room. There was a roach crawling high on the wall. He looked over to the window. A pale moon was shining in the sky. The chorus of crickets still came from the swamp. Jonas was sweating. He wondered what the book was going to tell next. He began to read once again.

The young man in the story sees a book by his bedstand. The title of the book is The Old Plantation. *He picks it up and begins to read. As he reads the first chapter, his face takes on a look of fear. Then, slowly, a look of understanding comes over his face.*

Jonas stopped reading again. He felt the skin crawling on the back of his neck. What was it that the man in the story understood? Why didn't *he* understand? Jonas's mind began to throb with a terrible anxiety. He went back to the book.

The young man continues to read The Old Plantation. *The more he reads, the more frightened he becomes. Finally, he finishes the book. Then the young man lays the book back down on the nightstand. He knows there is nothing he can do. Nothing he can do. . . . but wait. . . .*

Eagerly, Jonas turned to the next page of *The Old Plantation.* But the next page and the next page and the next page were blank. The rest of the book was blank. Jonas put it back on the nightstand.

Jonas lay in his bed and waited. He was shaking all over now. What was he waiting for?

Suddenly, Jonas was aware that the crickets had stopped and there was dead silence. In the moonlight, the trees looked frozen stiff. Everything seemed to have stopped.

Then, Jonas heard a car coming up the driveway toward the old plantation. He leaned over and blew out the candle beside his bed. He didn't know what to do but wait. He waited, without moving, while he heard the engine stop and the car door slam. He waited as he heard a key being put into the front door. He waited, trembling under the covers, while he listened to the footsteps going throughout the house, and then stopping in front of his bedroom.

Then, as the doorknob turned and the door opened, Jonas finally understood what he had been waiting for.

It was himself, standing in the doorway, looking at the clean little room. On the nightstand beside the bed he saw a partially burned candle and an old book. He smiled to himself, thinking he might read the book after a walk on the veranda.

Then Jonas Ellerby went to get his luggage from the car. He had decided to spend the night at the Old Plantation.

PHOBIA

Many people have a phobia — an unnatural fear they can't control, but Ellen's phobia bordered on the fringe of madness. She would go into hysteria even at the sight of a small fieldmouse. Perhaps she had a right to be afraid, after what happened that night.

It was twilight when Ellen left the small restaurant where she had eaten dinner, alone. The restaurant stood on one side of the large city park. And because it was a warm summer night, Ellen decided to walk through the park to her apartment on the other side.

She started down a path overhung by leafy trees. It was surprisingly dark on the path, dark enough to make Ellen feel uneasy. She quickened her pace, thinking she should get to the other side of the park as soon as possible. She had heard stories about things, unpleasant things, that happened to people in the park at night.

Then, coming out of the shaded path into an open area, she saw the sky was still light. She decided to walk a little slower, but she couldn't completely forget her uneasiness, or the stories.

She walked on through the park, toward the lake in the middle. Soon, another path loomed ahead, shaded by thick trees. Ellen looked in the distance down the path. No one seemed to be on it. She looked behind her, wondering if she should turn around. By now, though, she had walked into the center of the park. There was no point in turning back.

Once on the shaded path, she could hear no sounds but the rustle of leaves. The sounds of the city were drowned out here. Ellen walked on, listening to the leaves whispering in the night air. She felt as though she were a thousand miles from civilization. But then her ears picked up another sound. It wasn't a sound from the city outside and it wasn't a sound from the trees, either. She listened to her own footsteps on the cement path. She told herself that was what she had heard.

But no, she heard it again, an echo of her own footsteps behind her. She was sure of it now, there were other footsteps, following her. Fear crept into her mind. It made her heart pound and her legs walk faster.

Soon, Ellen knew she had reason to be afraid. The footsteps behind were keeping pace with hers; they had quickened with her own.

She kept herself from running, knowing she must not show her fear; she knew she must stay in control of herself. Forcing her legs to slow down, she realized the footsteps behind her were not slowing down. They came up from behind, quickly, eagerly.

Ellen couldn't control her fear any longer. She broke into a run down the path. The footsteps didn't follow right away. But then, over the pounding of her heart, she heard them hitting the pavement, fast and steady.

Ahead, Ellen saw the path that went down to the lake. She knew that people more often came to the lake than to any other place in the park. She ran down a small hill toward the lake. As she rounded a corner, her heart sank. The path by the lake was deserted, too. And, now, the footsteps behind her were coming down the hill and were catching up with her.

Ellen looked around wildly. There was a dense area of bushes and trees to her left. She ran on a few steps and then threw herself into hiding in the bushes. Maybe, she prayed, the footsteps would go by.

It was dark by now. Only a half moon penetrated the night with its mellow light. Ellen heard the footsteps first, then she saw the shadow that belonged to them.

The man stopped walking twenty feet from where she was hiding. He stood silent for a minute with his back to her. Then he walked over to a bench at the lake's edge. He sat down on it.

In the bushes, Ellen sat sweating. She wondered why she had ever stopped running. Nothing could be worse than this. The man must know she was hiding. Was he going to wait it out—until she couldn't stand to hide any longer? Then Ellen thought of a chance. Others might walk along the path. She would jump out of the bushes then and walk with them out of the park.

She looked over at the man on the bench again. He sat calmly looking out at the lake. Something caught her eye. There was a small shadow moving along the water's edge. It stopped. Silhouetted against the sky, Ellen could see the head of a large rat. She started to get up off the ground. That was always her reaction to mice—to stand on a chair, to get up off the floor in any way possible. But now, she couldn't get up. And she couldn't let loose the scream choking in her throat.

As in a bad nightmare, three more rats joined the one by the lake. Ellen could see their fat shadows and their ugly rodent heads in the moonlight. And she could hear the clatter of their claws on the cement path. She wanted to scream, she wanted to run. But the bigger shadow on the bench scared her more.

He sat still on the bench, the rats not more

than five feet away from him. He must see them, Ellen thought. What kind of man is he?

She switched her eyes back to the rats. They hypnotized her with loathing fear. She heard a rustle in the bushes, not more than two feet from her. She had to gag her mouth with her sweater to keep from screaming. What if a rat came up to her? What if it jumped on her with its sharp claws?

Then, with horror, Ellen saw that the four rats by the lake's edge were coming toward her. Their sharp rodent noses were pointing at her. Their long tails were switching back and forth.

Ellen screamed. She saw the shadow on the bench stand up. It started to come at her toward the bushes. She struggled to her feet. As she took a step backwards, her foot fell into a deep hole. It was a rat's nest. Dozens of baby rats squealed in panic and crawled out of the hole around her foot. They were everywhere, scuttling away in desperation. Ellen jerked her foot out of the hole. As she stepped back again, her foot landed on the soft body of a baby rat. It squealed in agony, and Ellen screamed and screamed again.

Then Ellen saw the shadow of the man moving closer and closer to her. She struggled to get out of the bushes, although her knees were weak with fear. Finally, she pushed her way through the thick branches and stepped onto the path going back up the hill.

The man had seen her. He came nearer. There, in the pale moonlight, Ellen saw his face. Her body was filled with revulsion. It was the face of a huge rat, its whiskers twitching.

Ellen ran. Terror, mindless terror, carried her down the path out of the park. She did not hear footsteps following behind her. All she heard was the high, unnatural squeal of rats.

Ellen ran on and on until she escaped finally, from the park. But the rat, she never really escaped him. He is still there . . . . in her mind.

THE TRAIN
THROUGH
TRANSYLVANIA

The train jerked to a halt in the foothills of Transylvania. Inside one of the small compartments, Stephanie Archer looked nervously out the window.

"I wonder what's the matter?" she asked. Her mother and brother, sitting across from her, both shrugged their shoulders.

"I'm glad it's still daylight," Stephanie said, looking out at the dense, green forest around them.

"Scared of vampires?" her brother asked.

"Oh, sure," Stephanie answered sarcastically.

"Well, then, you won't mind if I read to you from *Dracula*, will you? I thought it was fitting — us riding through Transylvania."

Mrs. Archer sighed, "Really, Robert."

Then, the slow grinding of the wheels against the track began again. Soon the train had picked up its normal speed.

Stephanie settled back against the old velvet seat and relaxed. Robert pulled a battered copy of Bram Stoker's *Dracula* from his knapsack. Mrs. Archer went on reading her novel. The three of them had the compartment, which could sit six, all to themselves.

Robert began to read aloud from *Dracula*.

"There lay the Count, but looking as if his youth had been half renewed, for the white hair and moustache were changed to dark iron-grey; the cheeks were fuller, and the white skin seemed ruby-red underneath; the mouth was redder than ever, for on the lips were gouts of fresh blood, which trickled from the corners of the mouth and ran over the chin and neck."

"Oh, stop it, Robert," Stephanie interrupted.

"I was just trying to set the mood for our journey," Robert protested. "Here we are in the heart of vampire country. We might as well enjoy it."

"Robert, stop reading aloud if it bothers Stephanie," Mrs. Archer insisted. "We'll be meeting your father in Bucharest tomorrow, thank goodness. Then I'm turning both of you over to him."

Robert picked up *Dracula* again and started to read, silently. Stephanie gazed out the window. The train was climbing out of a valley into the mountains.

"Listen to this!" Robert exclaimed and started to read aloud again:

"It seemed as if the whole awful creature were simply gorged with blood. He lay like a filthy leech . . ."

"Mother, make him stop it."

"I'll stop, I'll stop." Robert said hastily. "I didn't know you were so sensitive, Stephanie."

Just then, the train came to another halt. All three of them looked out to see where they were. A station sign read "Mehadia."

"Quite a few people are getting on . . ." Robert said, craning his head out the window.

"I hope no one comes in here," Stephanie said.

But a minute later, they heard footsteps in the corridor, and the door to their compartment slid open. A short, well-dressed, elderly man stuck his head inside.

"May I join you? I'm afraid the other compartments are full."

"Of course," Mrs. Archer said. "Please come in."

The elderly man sat down by the door, beside Stephanie.

"My name is Dr. Maurer. You are Americans, are you not?"

"Yes, that's right. I'm Mrs. Rita Archer. This is my daughter Stephanie and my son Robert."

The old man beamed a smile at everyone. "Very happy to meet you."

The train jerked forward and then began to pull out of the station.

"Where do you. . . ." Mrs. Archer began to say to the doctor. But she stopped as the compartment door slid open again.

A tall, middle-aged man walked into the compartment. He didn't say a word. Without hesitation, he walked to the window and sat down on the other side of Stephanie.

Stephanie glanced at the new man sitting beside her. She saw his black hair, white skin . . . and red lips. They *were* red, those lips, ruby-red.

Stephanie looked over to Robert. Robert met her gaze and raised his eyebrows. The second stranger's presence invaded the entire compartment. No one seemed to know what to say.

Stephanie moved over on the seat, closer to the old doctor. It had suddenly seemed to her that the dark stranger's body was cold — unnaturally cold. She started to shiver and couldn't stop.

"Robert, could you get me a sweater?"

"Ah . . . . sure, Steph." Robert stood up to get a sweater from the overhead rack. As he did, the copy of *Dracula* fell from his lap onto the floor, at the stranger's feet.

Robert stooped to pick it up. But the stranger already had it in his bony hand. He gave it back to Robert. There was a smirk on his face and his hard, black eyes looked deep into Robert's.

Robert sat down again, forgetting about the sweater. Mrs. Archer handed over her sweater to Stephanie. Then she said to the doctor, "It's always nice to have a doctor around." The old doctor smiled kindly.

Everyone settled back into an awkward silence. The strange man sat perfectly still beside Stephanie. As the light began to fade in the sky, his white face took on a greater contrast to his black hair and black suit. Stephanie cast quick glances at him as she pretended to stare intently out the window. She couldn't get the words from *Dracula* out of her mind. This man was so strange . . . and they *were* in Transylvania.

"Robert," Mrs. Archer said softly, "could you switch on the light, please. It's getting difficult to read."

As Robert reached up to flick on the light switch, the doctor reached over and touched his arm.

"Please, Mrs. Archer, wait a few more minutes with the light, if you don't mind. As a frequent traveler through these parts, I can recommend watching the countryside now. It is twilight, near sunset. The sky will be full of beautiful colors in the next half hour. You really shouldn't miss it."

"Of course, Doctor," Mrs. Archer agreed.

Stephanie leaned her head against the seat back. If only she could enjoy the countryside, she thought. But with that man so close to her. . . .

The train took a sharp turn and everyone was thrown to the right. The stranger's body pressed against Stephanie. She tried to move away, but her body was wedged between him and the doctor. The train straightened its course, but the man didn't move away from Stephanie. She turned to him. He was looking deep into her eyes. Just as she felt herself about to scream, he moved away from her.

The train was puffing to a slow stop at a small village called Orsova. Suddenly, unbelievably, the dark stranger got up and left the compartment — as quickly as he had entered it.

They watched him as he stepped onto the station platform and walked toward a young woman who was waiting there. As the train drew away from the station, they could see the two kissing.

Robert and Stephanie looked at each other and then started to laugh hysterically. Mrs. Archer smiled as she rearranged her things on the seat. The old doctor continued to smile at everyone.

"You two are ridiculous," Mrs. Archer said to Stephanie and Robert. "Stop giggling." But then she laughed herself.

"I think I'll go and wash up now," Mrs.

Archer said. She stood up and turned around to reach for her bag on the overhead rack. After she got it down, she stopped to check her face in the mirror. In the reflection behind her own face, she saw Stephanie sitting alone on the opposite seat.

"Why . . . where did the doctor . . ." she began to say. But when she did turn around, to her surprise, the doctor was still in his seat.

How odd, Mrs. Archer thought as the train plunged into another dark mountain tunnel. She sat back down again.

The shrill train whistle pierced through the air. The rattle of the wheels on the tracks echoed throughout the tunnel. No other sound could be heard in the pitch blackness of the compartment.

Three minutes later, the train shot back out into the velvet blue twilight.

"Stephanie!" Mrs. Archer shrieked.

Stephanie was slumped across the seat, her head thrown back. Blood dribbled from two small holes in her neck. An unnatural smile played on her lips.

"Doctor," she sighed.

But the doctor was gone.

And a full moon shone brilliantly in the Transylvanian sky.

THE
ATTIC DOOR

She pushed open the creaking, cast-iron gate in the fence that surrounded the house. It banged shut behind her as she walked up to the front door. Thick clumps of lilacs hung over the doorway; the air was laden with their suffocating sweet odor.

Rosalyn lifted the heavy brass knocker and then let it fall. A hollow thump echoed inside the house. A few seconds later, the door opened.

"Rosalyn, it is you, isn't it? You're so grown up, I hardly recognize you." Then she was smothered in the lilac-perfumed embrace of her aunt.

"Hello, Aunt Harriet."

"Come inside, dear, out of this humidity. The house always stays cool inside."

Rosalyn followed her aunt into a large, dark hallway that was as cool as an underground cave.

"Here you are, finally visiting me after sixteen years. How was your train ride?" But Aunt Harriet didn't wait for an answer; she chattered on. "I've been after your father to let you come for years. Well, it isn't any secret that your father didn't like my husband, is it? But now that dear Arthur has been dead for four years . . ." Aunt Harriet paused and then sighed. "It has been four long years since Arthur killed himself." Rosalyn stared down at her feet. She didn't know what to say. Her mother had warned her that Aunt Harriet might be a little strange. She was right.

"This is an enormous house, Aunt Harriet," Rosalyn finally said.

"I'll take you on a tour once you've had time to unpack. Now you must want to see your bedroom."

"See your bedroom," a strange voice croaked out.

"Who was that?" Rosalyn asked uneasily.

Aunt Harriet laughed her high, tittering laugh and walked over to the end of the hallway. She pulled off a green, velvet cover, revealing a large parrot in a cage.

"That was Polly, wasn't it, Polly?" Aunt Harriet made bird noises to the parrot.

Rosalyn didn't go over to the bird cage. She hated parrots. "Aunt Harriet, I think I'll go to my room now. If you could show me where it is. . . ."

"Of course, Rosalyn. . . . I'll be right back, Polly."

Aunt Harriet led the way up a curved flight of stairs leading to the second floor. She walked down to the room at the end of the hall.

"Here is your room, Rosalyn. I hope you like it. It used to be my sitting room when I was first married."

Rosalyn peeked inside. The entire room was done in lilac. The bedspread was bright lilac; the wallpaper was a design of pale lilac flowers on white. Even the furniture had been painted lilac.

"Oh, Aunt Harriet." That was all Rosalyn could think of to say.

"You get yourself settled in, Rosalyn dear. Then come down and we'll have tea together."

Twenty minutes later, Rosalyn came down the curving staircase to join her aunt for tea. Aunt Harriet was waiting in a sun-lit room off the main hallway. Tea and cake were already sitting on a small table by the sofa.

"Have some of my delicious cake, Rosalyn. It's so nice for me to have company. Polly and I have to eat alone, usually, don't we, Polly?"

"Alone," croaked Polly. Rosalyn saw that the parrot's cage had been set by the window.

Rosalyn ate some of the cake and sipped her tea. Her eyes slowly surveyed the room. The furnishings were very old-fashioned. The lamps had crystal beads hanging from the shades. Old velvet cloths edged with fringe were thrown over the chairs. Little statues and nicknacks and pictures were everywhere. One picture, in particular, caught Rosalyn's eyes. "Is that my cousin Herman?" she asked.

Aunt Harriet made a choking sound in her throat.

"I'm sorry, Aunt Harriet; that was rude of me." Rosalyn blushed. She knew that Aunt Harriet must feel awful about losing her son Herman when he was so young. And Uncle Arthur had killed himself just a month later. Rosalyn tried to make up for upsetting her aunt. "You know, Aunt Harriet, I always wished I had known Herman. We were born in the same year. I cried when I heard that he had died — even though I had never met him."

Aunt Harriet had regained her composure. "Yes dear, that is a picture of Herman. Now, let's not talk about the past. I want to show you the house."

Rosalyn followed her aunt out of the room and into the dark hallway again.

"First, I want to show you your Uncle Arthur's study and laboratory. Arthur was a great scientist, you know. He was just ahead of his time. The people at the university were jealous of his superiority. That was the only reason he had to leave and carry on his experiments at home."

They had walked into a huge book-lined room. Rosalyn looked around it in awe. So this was where Uncle Arthur worked. She had always known he was a scientist. But her father refused to talk about his work. She knew there had been some sort of scandal and Uncle Arthur had been dismissed from his university post.

"And through this door," Aunt Harriet said as she walked on, "is his laboratory."

The next room was even more awesome. It was filled with labeled jars of chemicals, test tubes, and other scientific equipment.

"Just what did Uncle Arthur study?" Rosalyn asked.

"He was a biologist, a great biologist," Aunt Harriet said in a reverent tone. "He studied human mutations."

"Oh," Rosalyn said. She looked around the walls. There were pictures of apes and monkeys hanging beside photographs of human bodies.

"You understand, don't you, Rosalyn, that you mustn't touch anything in these two rooms. They are a monument to my husband's greatness. Some day science will come to understand his genius. These rooms must be preserved exactly as they are."

"Yes, Aunt Harriet," Rosalyn said as she followed her aunt back through the study and into the hallway again.

"The rest of the house you can explore on

you own, Rosalyn," Aunt Harriet said. "But I want to make one thing very clear to you," Aunt Harriet's voice hardened, "I never want you to go up into the attic. Do you understand that?"

"Do you understand that?" the parrot mimicked from the next room.

"I'm very serious, Rosalyn. Never open the door that leads to the attic. Or you'll be sorry."

"You'll be sorry," Polly croaked out.

Rosalyn felt a strange sensation come over her. "I understand, Aunt Harriet," she promised.

Rosalyn spent the next days wandering about the house, leafing through the old books she found, and sitting out in the garden at night with her aunt. Aunt Harriet asked a lot of questions about Rosalyn's father and mother. But she changed the subject whenever Rosalyn asked more about her cousin Herman.

The time passed pleasantly enough for Rosalyn, but after a few days she became restless. There was no one else to talk to but Aunt Harriet. Rosalyn was ready for something to break the tedium.

The fourth day she was there, Aunt Harriet announced that she was going to a friend's house for afternoon tea. Rosalyn could come along if she wanted.

Rosalyn thought it over and decided she would probably be bored. She told her aunt she would stay home by herself, perhaps go out into the garden and read.

When her aunt left, Rosalyn went up to her room and tried to read a novel she had brought along. But the novel didn't interest her. After a few minutes, she slammed the book shut. She got up and went out into the hallway. There was nothing she could think of to do. Her vacation had turned out to be a disappointment.

As she walked down the hallway, she passed the door that she knew led up to the attic. She paused in front of it. Aunt Harriet had acted very strangely about her going into the attic. Rosalyn wondered what could be up there . . . Probably a lot of old clothes that Aunt Harriet didn't want her to to get into. Or maybe there were other family photographs that her aunt didn't want to have to talk about. Rosalyn put her hand on the doorknob. To her surprise, it turned. But then she took her hand away. Aunt Harriet had warned her, almost threatened her, not to go up there.

She started to walk away. But her curiosity about the attic made her stop. Aunt Harriet *was* a little crazy. There was probably no reason in the world why she shouldn't go up into the attic.

Making up her mind, Rosalyn put her hand on the doorknob again and turned it. As she pushed the door open, it stuck for a moment, but then swung open. A short flight of stairs led up to the attic. Rosalyn walked up them slowly. As her eyes reached the level of the attic floor, she saw something that brought her to a dead halt. She stared at the thing — the half human, half animal thing staring back at her. Then she left out an awful scream and scrambled back down the attic stairs.

Rosalyn felt sick. She couldn't believe what she had just seen. It didn't make any sense — it was some monstrous, living thing such as she had never before seen. She pushed open the attic door and ran to the stairway. Then she heard what she had feared. Steps were coming down the attic stairs behind her — the steps of that thing.

For a moment, Rosalyn's knees gave out. She tried to run away as she saw the thing come onto the hall landing, but she couldn't. The awful creature came nearer her. It reached out a fur-covered arm. Rosalyn ran.

She ran down the steps, nearly falling. The thing came after her. She could hear it making short, snorting sounds as it breathed. Rosalyn ran into the living room.

Then she realized in a second that there was no way out of the room. She dashed for the door again, just barely missing the thing's outstretched arm.

She ran down the hallway to the kitchen. The thing lumbered after her. She tried to

get its face out of her mind. It was the face—
the strangely human face—that bothered her
most. She ran through the kitchen to the back
door to the garden. Too late, she realized that
the garden, also, was a dead end.

Rosalyn pressed her back up against the
stone garden wall. The thing came out of the
back door and shuffled toward her. She saw
its ugly face spread wide in a smile. She
screamed and darted to one side. Again, she
just escaped its outstretched arm.

But now it was close behind her. Rosalyn
ran through the kitchen and into the hallway.
But she didn't make it to the front door. She
stumbled and fell.

The thing came up and stood over Rosalyn.
It reached its furry arm down to her and
tapped her on the head.

"Tag, you're it," it said in a human voice.

"Tag, you're it," the parrot croaked from its
cage.

Rosalyn fainted.

When she came to, the thing's face was
still hovering over her. But beside it was Aunt
Harriet's face.

"Rosalyn, you naughty girl. What did I
tell you about going into the attic. I said you
would be sorry." Aunt Harriet was shaking
her finger at Rosalyn. "You've got poor Herman all nervous now."

"Poor Herman," the parrot repeated.

"Yes, poor Herman," Aunt Harriet said, stroking her son's head. "He has never been the same since Arthur's last experiment."

Then Aunt Harriet looked down at Rosalyn again. "You do realize, Rosalyn, that we can't let you go now. Not now that you know our secret. I'll call your parents and tell them that you never arrived here. And we can arrange a nice room for her in the attic, can't we Herman?"

Rosalyn looked up into her mad aunt's face. Then she looked at her cousin. An eager grin was spread across Herman's ugly face.

"You'll be very happy with us, Rosalyn," Aunt Harriet said.

"Very happy," the parrot croaked.

Rosalyn screamed. And then she fainted away again.

Herman picked up her limp body and started carrying it up the staircase to the attic door.

THE TUNNEL
OF TERROR

In the late summer, just before school started, Ellen always went to the Ohio State Fair with her friends. This year she set off for the state capital early one hot, summer morning with her friends, Jane and Diane. They laughed and talked all the way to Columbus on the two-hour trip. Arriving at the fair, they joined the crowd of people circling the dusty midway lined with food stands, rides, and other amusements.

By late afternoon, the three of them were tired and a little bored. They had seen nothing new from last year. Still, they decided to walk around the midway just one more time.

They passed the ice cream and hot dog and waffle stands. They looked over the Ferris wheel, the Wild Mouse and all the other rides again. And they walked by the freak show advertisements showing the fat lady, the Siamese twins, and the man with a rubber mouth.

Then they passed a small passageway they hadn't noticed before. Ellen suggested they follow it to see what was at the end. The passage twisted around behind the canvas tents until it ended at a huge sign advertising something called The Tunnel of Terror. The sign showed a small boat traveling along a dark canal. Along one side of the canal was a scene with wax figures showing someone being guillotined in the French Revolution.

"Creepy," Jane said. "I wouldn't go in there."

Ellen wasn't sure what put the idea into her head, but suddenly she wanted to ride through the Tunnel of Terror. Maybe it was that the tunnel looked cool and she was weary of the searing heat of the midway. Or maybe it was that she was looking for something new in her life, some new experience that would be strange and different.

"Anybody dare me to go in?" she asked.

"Are you crazy?" Diane said.

"I dare you," Jane said.

"All right, I'll go," Ellen announced bravely. "I suppose you two are afraid."

"We'll pay your way, right, Diane?" Jane said. "But wild horses couldn't drag me in there."

The three walked up the ticket booth. A grizzled old man sat in it, cleaning his fingernails with a penknife.

"One, please," Ellen said.

"You're going in alone, are you?" the old man asked, staring at her through his bushy eyebrows.

"I'm not afraid," Ellen said. "Where do I catch the boat?"

The old man motioned her behind the ticket booth. As she went around, Diane and Jane started to follow.

"No," the old man said, "you can't go any further. You didn't buy tickets."

Ellen tried to sound cheerful as she yelled good-bye to her friends. But the boat was old and creaking, and she shivered as she slipped into the moldy, leather seat.

The old man pulled a wooden handle beside the canal that started a gear in motion. Ellen was startled by the noise and turned around to look at him. His mouth was set in a wide grin that showed his dirty, decaying teeth. Then, suddenly, she saw nothing; the boat had glided into pitch-black darkness.

In the dark, Ellen noticed that her sense of hearing became very keen. There was the creaking drag of the boat along the canal. There was the slobbering lap of the water against the sides of the boat. Then there was a shriek that made her heart jump to her throat.

A second after the shriek, a spotlight flashed on. Two feet in front of the boat was a man stretched out on a torture rack, his arms tearing from their sockets. Ellen could see the red blood oozing from his skin. She closed her eyes and buried her face in her hands. How much longer would this last?

The boat jerked around a sharp turn. Then the shriek Ellen heard was her own. A slimy mass had just passed over her face. She crouched down in the boat, feeling sick to her stomach. If she could stay like this until the trip was over, maybe she could stand it. Why did she ever want to come in here, she asked herself. She would give anything to be out in the bright sunlight with her friends.

There was a rumbling sound in front of her. Then Ellen heard the sharp hit of metal against wood. She peeked from between her hands. It was the guillotine scene. A bloody head rolled from the victim's head into a bucket next to the guillotine's sharp blade.

She braced herself for the next scene as the boat took another sickening, sharp turn. She felt something wet, something furry, slip around her shoulders. She tried to contain her screams. It would go away, she told herself, just like the slimy mass before. But the wet fur seemed to press closer to her. She felt a weight get into the boat beside her. She screamed and screamed and screamed. . . .

Outside, Jane and Diane were laughing about the noises coming from inside the Tunnel of Terror. They could see that the old man was enjoying it, too. He leered at them, with a strange grin on his face.

But then, the noise from the Tunnel of Terror seemed to change. The screaming became constant, taking on a shrill tone of madness. The two girls looked at each other uneasily. Jane walked up to the old man's ticket booth.

"Will she be coming out soon?" she asked him.

"In another few minutes," he answered, still grinning. "Getting her money's worth, ain't she?"

Jane walked back to where Diane stood at the end of the canal. "I don't like it. I wish she would come out."

Just then the air was split with a cry of terror so awful the two girls shuddered at the sound of it.

"Get her out of there!" Jane said, running up to the old man.

"Nothing I can do," he said.

The screaming went on in the tunnel. It was hysterical now. Then a louder sound pierced the air. An announcement was being made over the intercom of the fair grounds.

"Ladies and gentleman. It is important that you stay calm and don't panic. A gorilla has escaped from the zoo. Please find a safe place to wait until it has been recaptured. Don't go anywhere alone. Let me repeat again, don't panic."

But the announcement came too late for

Ellen. Her friends watched as she glided out of the tunnel, the gorilla sitting on the seat beside her.

They got Ellen out of the boat. And, miraculously, she was unharmed. Except for her mind, that is.

They had to take her to the state hospital in Pleasant Valley immediately.

THE
FORTUNE-TELLER

Mr. Peebles pushed aside the curtain of glass beads that hung over the entrance to the fortune-teller's chamber. He walked inside. Behind him, the beads swung back together with a clatter.

Mr. Peebles was alone in the chamber. He sat down on a chair and surveyed the room. Red and black silk curtains hung all around the walls, alternating in color. The floor was covered with brightly designed Persian carpets. Mr. Peebles looked up. Painted on the black ceiling were symbols and pictures which he had never seen before. An eerie blue light shone throughout the room.

Mr. Peebles put his hands on his knees and waited. His wife had told him that he would have to wait. It was his wife, in fact, who had persuaded Mr. Peebles to come to the fortune-teller. Mr. Peebles himself was a far too reasonable man to be interested in hocus-pocus like this, but his wife was a persuasive woman.

The swishing sound of silk against silk made

Mr. Peebles look up. The fortune-teller had entered the chamber. She was a large woman with long, black hair. Her costume was flamboyant. The red, full dress was adorned with necklaces, bangles, and a silver belt which had a clasp designed of two intertwined snakes' heads.

"You are Mr. Peebles." The fortune-teller announced this as a fact, not a question.

"Yes, yes, I am," Mr. Peebles stammered, suddenly flustered by the presence of this overwhelming woman.

"Take my hand and come to the table." The woman reached a heavily-bangled arm out to Mr. Peebles. He drew his arm out to her and she clutched his hand tightly, almost fiercely. She led him over to one corner of the room where a round table sat. Two chairs were arranged around it, opposite from each other.

"Sit down, Mr. Peebles, and we will begin." Mr. Peebles stumbled into the chair to which the fortune-teller pointed and sat down. His eyes were riveted on the crystal ball which sat in the dead center of the round table. He looked at it with a mixture of amusement and fear.

The chamber was much as he had expected. It contained all the typical furnishings and paraphernalia of the fortune-teller. And, yet, he was uneasy here. His common sense was disturbed by the presence of this woman, who already exerted a magnetic influence over him.

"Look into my eyes, Mr. Peebles." The fortune-teller's voice was strong and suggestive. Mr. Peebles obeyed.

"You have suffered a great misfortune, haven't you, Mr. Peebles?" she said, staring deep into his eyes.

"Yes, that's right . . ." Mr. Peebles began.

"You lost the job you had for twenty years, didn't you, Mr. Peebles?"

Now it seemed to Mr. Peebles that the fortune-teller could see behind his eyes, into his brain.

"How did you know?" he asked dreamily.

"I know," the fortune-teller replied. "And I know more. You fear death, don't you, Mr. Peebles? You feel the hand of death tightening around your neck."

At that moment, Mr. Peeble's neck did seem to be choked by an invisible hand. He began to pour out what had been haunting him these past months.

"Yes, I fear death, yes. I feel that life has passed me by and that all that is left for me is death."

"Poor Mr. Peebles," the fortune-teller's voice went on soothingly. "Let me consult the crystal ball."

The fortune-teller led Mr. Peebles' gaze from her eyes down to the crystal ball. It radiated an intense blue light — the eerie blue glow that Mr. Peebles had noticed in the room earlier.

The fortune-teller began to drone a rhythmic chant as she stared into the crystal ball. Then, suddenly, she sucked in her breath. Mr. Peebles shifted his eyes from the crystal ball to her face. Her eyes were burning and the black brows were knit together.

"I see doom before you, Mr. Peebles. What the crystal ball has told me is not pleasant. It gives a black picture of your future. Death . . ."

Her words were drowned out by Mr. Peebles' shriek of despair. His fears had been right. Death was stalking him.

He felt the fortune teller's fingers entwine in his. "Mr. Peebles, Mr. Peebles. We all must die. You must simply accept it . . . and provide for your loved ones."

Mr. Peebles came out of his reverie. Loved ones, yes, he must provide for his beloved wife, Margaret . . . his darling Margaret.

Mr. Peebles left the fortune-teller's chamber in a daze. He stumbled from the dark room penetrated by the eerie blue light out into the darker blackness of the winter night. As he drove his car home, he made himself a promise. No matter what came to him and how soon, he would take care of Margaret.

Margaret was standing in the hallway, waiting for him, when he arrived home. To a stranger, they would have appeared to be father and daughter. She was, in fact, fifteen years younger than her husband.

"Margaret, it's awful. She said just what I feared . . ." Mr. Peebles poured out his experience with the fortune-teller to his wife. She listened to his story, stroking his balding head with her soft hands.

"Margaret, you will be cared for. Don't worry. I plan to take out a $100,000 life insurance policy."

"Whatever you want, dear. But stop this horrible talk of death. I won't hear it any more. You laughed when I first suggested that you go to a fortune-teller. And now you take her silly prediction so seriously. . . ."

Mr. Peebles felt better after that. He and his wife went to bed.

The first thing Mr. Peebles did the next morning was to visit his insurance broker. Despite the broker's advice to the contrary, he insisted that he take out a new insurance policy immediately. The beneficiary would be, of course, his wife.

Mr. Peebles felt much better as he drove home from the insurance office, despite the meaning of what he had just done. He fell into a daydream about Margaret, how she could always keep the house, and live as she did now. . . .

SCREETCH. Mr. Peebles' foot trembled on the brake pedal. The train engine flashed before him, followed by a constant whiz of box cars. Their rumbling wheels on the track kept time with Mr. Peebles' pounding heart.

The fortune-teller had been right about death. He had just barely escaped it.

When he got home, Mr. Peebles told his wife about the train. She lay down on the couch and sobbed. To comfort her, he brought out the insurance policy. He kept repeating to her how she would always be protected.

That afternoon Mr. Peebles went out into the garage where he did small projects with wood to keep himself busy. Now he needed to get his mind off the morning incident with the train. He cleaned off the worktable area, putting tools back in their proper drawers. There seemed to be a knife he had misplaced.

He rummaged through more drawers. Then, he reached up to a cabinet high above the table. As he pulled the door open, the missing knife fell from the cabinet ledge. Its sharp blade plunged down an inch away from his terrified eyes. The knife dug into the wooden workbench and vibrated from the force of its impact. Mr. Peebles backed away in horror.

There was a death jinx on him.

Mr. Peebles spent the rest of the afternoon lying on the couch in his study. He was paralyzed with fear. Death's bony hand seemed to be tightening its grip around his neck. He refused the dinner his wife brought him. He refused even to talk with her. Finally, in the late evening, he felt that he must get out of the house. He decided to take a walk along a deserted road near the house. He would be safe there. No traffic was allowed on the path.

"Margaret," he called out to his wife. "I'm going to take a walk on the Old Mill Road. I'll be a while. Please don't wait up for me."

Margaret came into the room and watched her husband dress for his walk.

"You'll be careful, won't you? Remember what the fortune-teller said."

"Yes, I'll be careful, Margaret." Mr. Peebles kissed his wife's lips. "I'll see you later," he said as he went out the door.

Margaret waited until she heard the door shut. Then, with a smile on her face, she walked over to the telephone.

Along the path that was once the Old Mill Road, Mr. Peebles shuffled his feet through the dead autumn leaves. He let memories of his life drift in and out of his mind. It seemed so peaceful on the path. Mr. Peebles began to think that the fortune-teller might be wrong.

Then, he was blinded by two headlights. Speeding toward him, straight down the middle of the old path, was a huge car. He knew immediately that this was the end. Death had him in a stranglehold at last.

Mr. Peebles stared at death as it bore down on him. In the seconds before he died, he saw the face that death wore. It was the face of the fortune-teller behind the wheel of the car. And, on the dashboard in front of her, was the crystal ball.

THE
STUFFED DOG

The stuffed dog sat on a low table in the darkest corner of the study. It was a black boxer with short bristly hair that was still sleek. Mrs. Heathcote dusted it every week and rubbed oil into its hair every month. She took good care of the boxer in remembrance of her husband, the late Mr. Heathcote. He and the dog had died on the same day, twenty years ago.

The dog had been devoted to Mr. Heathcote. Mrs. Heathcote liked to think it had died out of grief at its master's death. The coroner, however, didn't find that a satisfactory explanation. Mr. Heathcote, you see, had died a very mysterious death. And when the boxer died the same day, the coroner had naturally been suspicious. He ordered an autopsy of both bodies—Mr. Heathcote's and the dog's. But no medical cause for either death had been determined.

Mrs. Heathcote buried her husband and

had the boxer stuffed. It had sat in that corner of the study for twenty years. Except, that is, on one day of each year — the anniversary of Mr. Heathcote's death. On that day, Mrs. Heathcote would lift the stuffed dog into her arms, carry him to the car, and drive with him beside her on the front seat to the cemetery. There, she would lay the dog on top of her husband's grave. She would smile to herself, imagining that the three of them were all together again.

This year, Mrs. Heathcote had asked her grandson, Theodore, to help her carry the dog to the cemetery. She was having back trouble, and the stuffed dog was heavy.

Theodore was twelve. He had never met his grandfather and he didn't understand why his grandmother took the stuffed animal to the cemetery every year. But, at his mother's insistence, he agreed to spend this weekend with his grandmother. He arrived early Saturday morning, the day of the pilgrimage to the cemetery.

"Teddy, you're so grown up," Mrs. Heathcote said as she squeezed Theodore up against her, just as she had always done. Theodore drew away from his grandmother. He noticed that his glasses had become smeared by something on her apron. As he pulled out his handkerchief and started to clean his glasses, he said, "Don't call me Teddy."

"Yes, Theodore, I'll try to remember," Mrs. Heathcote said apologetically. "Now come along and help me with the dear doggie. It looks like it may rain today so we must be off to the cemetery right away."

Theodore followed his grandmother into the house. He began to wish he hadn't let his mother persuade him to come. As he walked into the study, he felt the revulsion creep into his body. It was the same revulsion he had always felt toward this room. He despised the stuffed dog.

As a child he had been locked in this room once by his grandmother as punishment. He had sat in the room in the slowly fading light until it was pitch black. And during that whole time, the stuffed dog had stared at him with its beady eyes. He remembered how the cruel snarl on the dog's lips had haunted him in nightmares for weeks after. He remembered how the dog had filled him with a sinister feeling of fear. It was dead, and yet it seemed not dead.

"Teddy . . . I mean, Theodore, pick the dog up," his grandmother said.

Theodore walked over to the dog. But the idea of touching it made him sick.

"Really, Theodore, we must hurry. Lift the dog from the table."

Theodore put his hands on the stuffed dog. Its greasy fur felt unnatural to him. He lifted it from the table and carried it to the car as fast as he could. He set it on the front seat. His grandmother came out of the house as he started to get into the back seat.

"No, Teddy, sit in front with me and the dog — there's plenty of room."

As usual, Theodore obeyed. He moved the stuffed dog over on the seat toward his grandmother.

They were silent on the drive to the cemetery. Mrs. Heathcote seemed wrapped up in memories, and Theodore found the whole situation too ridiculous to talk about. He wondered if his grandmother was going batty.

Mrs. Heathcote stopped the car near her husband's grave.

"Teddy . . . Theodore, bring the dog now."

Theodore picked up the dog again. Its face stared up at him, the mouth fixed in that awful snarl.

Following his grandmother's directions, Theodore lay the dog on top of his grandfather's grave. He asked to be excused then. He wanted to get away from his grandmother and the dog and the creepy feeling he had from being around them.

After a half hour of walking around the cemetery, Theodore came back to his grandfather's grave. His grandmother's eyes were red and swollen from crying, but her face was beaming with a smile.

"Isn't it lovely, Teddy, seeing the two together like that?"

Theodore looked up with disgust at the stuffed dog lying on the grave.

"Is it time to go now?" he asked.

"Yes, dear, bring the dog back to the car."

Theodore bent down and picked up the dog. Then he let it fall back onto the grave.

"Theodore, what's wrong with you?" Mrs. Heathcote asked angrily.

But Theodore didn't know what to say. He didn't know how to tell her that the dog seemed warm now—as if it were alive. He fought the sickening disgust that he felt and stooped down to pick it up again. Yes, the dog was warm.

After he got the dog back into the car, Theodore went into the back seat and refused to move up front. During the ride home, all he could think of was having to pick the dog up again.

When they arrived home, Theodore gritted his teeth and carried the dog into the house. He never looked at the animal. He set it down in the study and then rushed out of the room.

Mrs. Heathcote watched him, shaking her head. "My, my, Theodore, you certainly are acting strange today. You young people haven't any sense, do you?"

Theodore wanted to leave his grandmother's house, but he had no choice. His mother had promised he would stay overnight. Theodore vowed never to go into that study again.

He passed the afternoon reading. While he

was eating his grandmother's delicious supper, he was almost happy he had stayed. The two of them settled down to play checkers after the dishes were washed.

They played checkers for two hours. Theodore let his grandmother win one game.

"You've tired me out, Theodore," Mrs. Heathcote declared sleepily after losing her fifteenth game. "Be a good boy and fetch the matches from the mantel in the study. I want to light a candle in your room tonight. I want it to be just like when your mother was little."

Mrs. Heathcote began her slow walk up the stairs to the bedrooms. "Bring the matches up when you come to bed, Teddy."

Theodore looked around the living room for a pack of matches. But he couldn't find any. There weren't any matches in the kitchen drawers, either. Finally, he walked up to the study door. He opened it and looked inside. It was too dark to see anything, even the dog. He decided to get the matches without turning the light on. He knew exactly where the mantel was in the room.

He slipped into the room and felt along the wall until his hand reached the mantel. His fingers closed around the match box. Just then, he thought he heard a noise from the corner of the room. A noise like a growl.

Theodore struck one of the matches against the box. In the burst of light from the match, he saw the dog's beady eyes looking at him.

A wave of hatred come over Theodore. That cursed dog.

With the match trembling in his hand, Theodore walked toward the stuffed dog. He looked at the fat jowls sagging around the cruel mouth. He stared into the beady eyes. As he came nearer to the dog, he saw its long whiskers.

Theodore laughed and shoved the match into those ugly whiskers. . . .

Upstairs, Mrs. Heathcote was putting on her nightrobe when she heard the scream. It was a horrible, terrified scream. She rushed down the steps as fast as her old legs would carry her. She hurried into the study.

Theodore was lying on the floor. His face had a look of terror on it. His arms and legs were sticking out stiff from his body.

"Oh no, oh no . . . not again. . . ." Mrs. Heathcote panted as she ran to call the doctor.

The doctor came within ten minutes. But that didn't matter. Theodore was already dead. The doctor said there would have to be an autopsy. Mrs. Heathcote nodded her head in agreement.

"He looks so much like my husband when he died," she said wistfully to herself.

They carried Theodore out of the study. And once again, the room was left in darkness.

Then a low snarl came from the corner. And a drop of bloody saliva fell from the stuffed dog's mouth.

A FREE PLACE
TO SLEEP

It was 2:00 a.m. in London, England. Tom and Dave were wandering through the streets like two sleepwalkers. They had inquired at hotel after hotel. None had vacancies. Now their footsteps echoed eerily through the empty, narrow streets of the city.

"I thought London didn't have fogs anymore," Dave grumbled. During the last hour, a foggy mist had been settling over the city. It was getting difficult for them to see the hotel signs, and harder yet to see the street signs.

"I've got to find some place to lie down," Tom moaned. "I don't care where; I just can't go any farther."

But go on they did, straining their eyes through the fog to find a place to stay. They walked from Picadilly Circus to Green Park. Then they headed north to Oxford Street. As they were walking down a street lined with old four-story buildings, they saw a sign. It was hanging on the black iron fence in front of the building. "For Sale," it read.

"Listen, I've got an idea," Tom said. "This place is probably vacant. What do you say we break in here and sleep for the night?"

"I'm ready to try anything," Dave answered.

The iron fence had sharp spikes on the top. The two climbed over the fence carefully, putting their feet on the iron crossbars and then leaping over the spiked points. It was a tricky thing to do, tired as they were.

Once over the fence, they tiptoed up to the front of the building. Through one of the windows, they could see that the rooms were being remodeled.

"It's empty, just as I thought," Tom whispered.

"Yeah, but how are we going to get in?" Dave asked.

Tom reached into his pocket and pulled out his Swiss Army knife. He wedged the knife between the top and bottom window and turned the old brass lock. Then he pushed the bottom section open. Tom looked at Dave with a smug grin of satisfaction.

The two boys hoisted themselves up onto the window ledge and then climbed into the room.

"I don't want to sleep here," Dave said, looking around the room. "Too many nails and tools lying around."

"OK, we'll check out the other rooms," Tom said.

They went out into the hallway of the old house. The cramped stair twisted upwards like the stairs in an old Amsterdam canal house. Tom started up and Dave followed. On the second floor, they tried the doors on all of the rooms. Everything was bolted. They climbed up to the third floor. Again, all the rooms were bolted shut.

"Looks like there is one more floor," Tom said, looking up the staircase. "Let's go."

They trudged up the final flight of stairs wearily. Dave was starting to complain again about being tired.

On the top landing there was only one door. The roof slanted steeply in on all sides. Tom tried the door knob. To his relief, it opened.

The two boys entered the small room. In it were two single beds and a dresser. A window overlooked the street below.

"Not bad," Tom said. He walked over to a stand and lit the candle that stood on it. Dave fell down on one of the old beds in exhaustion.

Just then, a loud bang echoed up the staircase from below them.

Dave jumped up. "What was that?"

Tom crept out into the hallway and stood there for a minute. Then he came back into the room.

"I think it was just the window we came in. It fell shut. We forgot to close it, didn't we?"

"Oh, yeah," Dave said, sitting down on one of the beds again. "This place gives me the creeps, though."

"Come on," Tom said. "It's a free place to sleep, isn't it?"

They both lay down on the beds. Tom lit a cigarette and then reached over and blew out the candle. As the light was extinguished, a weird cackle, almost like a laugh, seemed to come from the ceiling.

"Was that you, Tom?" Dave asked, sitting up in his bed.

"No," Tom said, his voice uneasy. "I think it was just something on the roof."

"Maybe we should get out of here, don't you think?" Dave asked.

Tom leaned back down in his bed. "And go where?"

They both were quiet for awhile.

"I mean, maybe this place is haunted or something," Dave said in the darkness.

"Be quiet and go to sleep."

Dave stopped talking, but then something else broke the silence. It was the sound of feet, moving up and down the staircase. But the feet were moving faster than any human feet ever could. The footsteps seemed to slide, to slither, to glide, up and down the stairs.

"I want to get out of here," Dave insisted in a panicked voice.

"OK, let's go." Tom jumped out of bed and lit the candle.

Just then, doors started slamming downstairs, the doors that had been locked before. And that weird cackle came again, this time from the hallway.

"I'm afraid to go out there, now," Dave said to Tom. He looked scared.

"Yeah, maybe we better stay in here." Tom walked over to the door. There was an iron bolt on it. He slid the bolt across the door frame. "Nobody's going to get in through here."

Tom went back and sat down on his bed. He tried to avoid Dave's eyes. He could tell that Dave was freaking out. He didn't feel so brave himself.

"Listen, we're OK," he said.

There was a rattling sound from the door. The two boys' eyes were fixed on the doorknob. It was moving back and forth.

"No, no, no . . ." Dave was shaking with fright on his bed.

"At least the bolt is there," Tom said to himself.

But then, by its own will, it seemed, the bolt slid back from the door frame. The two boys watched with horror as the door slowly, ever so slowly, moved open. After a few inches it stopped. There was dead silence.

Then the cackle, the weird sick cackle, penetrated the room. And through the narrow opening in the door, a shapeless green blob began to ooze.

Dave was frozen against the wall at the head of his bed. Tom jumped up and stood in a corner.

More of the blob oozed in. It was like slimy green jelly. It had a smell of evil. Then, suddenly, a head appeared out of the green ooze. The head had a horrible face, a face covered with knife wounds. The cackle came from the face. Then, as suddenly as it had appeared, the head disappeared back into the green blob.

On the bed, Dave was making choking sounds in his throat. He was trying to scream but couldn't. The blob oozed through the air toward him. It seemed drawn on by his fear.

Standing in the corner, Tom saw his chance to escape. He moved slowly against the wall until he was near the door. Then he ran for it. As he passed near the blob, he felt something cold and slimy swish along his arm. He turned back to see Dave's face staring at him. It had the look of death on it.

Tom ran harder. He almost fell down the steps to the front room. The window there, the window they had climbed in, was still open. He jumped out of it. Then he hurtled himself across the spiked fence. On the street, he looked up at the attic room. He couldn't see anything, but the weird cackle floated down to him.

Tom didn't know what to do. He ran out into the foggy street. He stopped for a moment.

Then, behind him, he heard Dave scream in agony.

Tom started running again. He ran until he came to St. James Park. Then he still kept running and running.

LONDON, 21 June — Early this morning, police found the body of 18-year-old Dave Moore impaled on the spiked fence in front of 50 Berkeley Square. The fourth-story window of the house was gaping open. Homicide detectives believe the young American was pushed from the small attic room. His traveling companion, 18-year-old Tom Dodd, is being sought for questioning. Suicide was ruled out because the victim's body showed signs of a struggle. Although 50 Berkeley Square has long been known as a "haunted" house, the homicide squad told reporters that "Scotland Yard does not believe in ghosts."

THE GOONEY BIRDS

They had been canoeing for five days in the wilderness. The four younger boys were hungry, sore, and totally exhausted. Jake, the guide, kept pushing them on. There was another portage just ahead.

"I don't think I can make it," Ty said in a weary voice. He shared a canoe with Ron. Ron didn't say anything, he just kept paddling. As usual, their canoe was lagging behind the other two.

Ahead, in the next canoe, Pete was working hard to keep up with his older brother Phil. He didn't want to look like a sissy in front of Phil — especially since he had persuaded Phil to take him and his friends on this canoe trip.

In the lead canoe, Jake paddled on with his smooth, strong strokes. Eric shared this canoe. Eric tried to do everything exactly as Jake did.

As their canoe glided within a few feet of the land, Jake leaped out into the water. Eric followed him a few seconds later. They guided the boat onto the shore and then pulled it out of the lake, watching for sharp rocks in the shallow water.

Several minutes later, Phil and Pete went through the same process. The four of them waited for Ty and Ron to come to shore. It wasn't unusual for them to have to wait. Ty and Ron were always five to ten minutes behind.

"Get a move on it, you two," Jake called out. "You're slowing us down." Jake liked to push on as fast as he could.

The canoe skimmed into the shoreline. Ron jumped out into the water to guide it in. In the back, Ty struggled awkwardly to leap out of the boat. He jumped into the water, and then lost his footing. While Ron pulled the boat up onto land, Ty floundered around in the water. Finally he waded out, totally drenched.

The others laughed at him. "You'll make a good target for the mosquitoes," Jake said. "At least you're good for something."

Eric laughed his high, whining laugh. He always laughed loudest at Jake's jokes.

"Let's go," Phil said, hoisting their canoe on his shoulders. Jake and Ron carried the other two canoes. Pete, Eric, and Ty carried the supplies.

The portage was a long one. Jake said it would take over an hour. The six of them tramped through the spongy undergrowth of the woods. The water squished in their leather boots with each step. They had all pulled down their mosquito nets to cover their faces and necks. But their hands and forearms were unprotected. The black northern mosquitoes buzzed around their bodies, thirsty for blood. It wasn't so bad for the supply carriers. They could slap the bugs away. But carrying the canoes required a tight grip of both hands. Jake cursed as he watched the welts rise on his arms. Ty stumbled along some way behind the rest. He stopped every few yards to swat away the mosquitoes that circled his body in a swarm.

"Look over there, in the crook of that tree," Phil yelled. "It's a gooney bird nest."

Everyone looked in the direction Phil's arm was pointing. There was a huge nest with large gray eggs in it. Gooney bird eggs.

"OK, you guys, it won't be the last time you see a gooney bird nest. Let's get going," Jake ordered, without breaking his stride.

They continued the rest of the portage in silence. When they came to the next lake, Jake pushed his canoe into the water and Eric loaded in the supplies.

"I thought we were going to have lunch now," Ty complained in the whimpering voice the others had grown to hate.

"On the next portage," Jake said without consulting anyone else.

"I'm starving, too," Ron said under his breath. But he pushed the canoe out into the lake, trying to catch up with the others who were already out ahead.

The three canoes moved out over the blue, clear lake. There was no conversation. Each person was either lost in his thoughts or too worn out by his physical exertion. The air was still.

Then, the silence was broken. The hoarse, croaking call of the gooney bird echoed over the lake. Seconds later, a huge bird dove down from the sky like a kamikaze bomber. Its body shot into the water, not more than twenty feet from the last canoe.

"That one came close," Ty leaned forward and whispered to Ron. He didn't like the gooney birds — in fact, he was afraid of them.

The two boys watched for the gooney bird to reappear. It took over a minute. Then it surfaced, several yards away from where it had entered the water. A silver fish was clamped in its strong beak.

The six canoeists watched as it took flight again. Ten minutes later, another hoarse croak came from in the sky. It was loud, incredibly loud. Everyone looked up. Even Jake couldn't believe his eyes.

"That's the biggest gooney bird I've ever seen," he exclaimed.

No one took his eyes from the bird. Its body straightened out like an arrow, ready for the dive. When it hit the water, waves rippled out that slapped against the canoes.

"A bird like that could kill you if it wanted to," Phil said in a quiet voice. Pete looked around to Ty and Ron. He had the same scared look on his face that they did.

The gooney bird resurfaced farther away from their canoes. But they could see its prey wriggling desperately in its beak.

No more gooney birds dove around them on the lake. They reached the next portage. After getting an OK from Jake, they pulled out the squashed loaves of bread and the peanut butter and jelly from their packs. It wasn't much food, hungry as they were, but they couldn't eat a lot until the evening meal, when they made camp.

The six sat silently, wolfing down their sandwiches. Ty finished first. He reached for more bread. Jake grabbed his arm as his hand went into the bread wrapper.

"You've had your share. That's all you get today. This food has to get us all the way back to base camp."

Ty withdrew his hand. Jake's grip had left marks on his arm.

The others started talking about the day's journey as Ty sat alone, feeling sorry for himself.

"You've been in this part before, haven't you, Jake?" Eric asked.

Jake said, arrogantly, "Not where we're going today."

"But I thought you said . . ." Phil began.

"I know, I know, I told you we'd go the regular route. But I've done that a million times. I thought I had a good group here." He stopped and sniggered, "That was before I found out about Ty." Then he continued his explanation. "Anyway, I decided last week that I'd go somewhere new. Somewhere that canoe parties don't go to."

"Great," Pete said without enthusiasm. He was too tired to feel adventurous.

Phil stood up. "Let's get moving, then." He felt a little worried. He had hired Jake and he was responsible for everyone else. But as long as Jake knew where he was going. . . .

They started the portage. Jake took the lead canoe again. But this time Pete and Ty shouldered the canoes while Phil and Ron and Eric carried supplies. Eric broke a trail through the woods, directed by Jake.

"Hey, look at this," Eric called out after they had been walking for twenty minutes.

The rest of them came to a halt around Eric. He had found another gooney bird nest. And it was filled by two pearly-gray eggs. But these eggs were unlike the others they had seen. They were huge. Too huge, almost, to belong to the same kind of bird.

"I want to go back," Ty whimpered. The huge eggs had set his imagination wild. In his mind, he could see a giant bird swooping down on him.

Eric laughed at him. "What's wrong with you, Ty, you scared of these eggs?" Eric walked over to the nest and took his walking stick and poked at it.

"Leave them alone, Eric," Phil ordered.

But Eric was looking at Jake, to see what Jake thought. Jake was smiling at him.

Eric took his stick in both hands and raised it high in the air. Then he drove it down, like a stake, first into one of the gooney bird eggs, and then into the other.

The others watched him do it in hushed silence. Then, high above them in the trees, there was a rustle of wings. An agonized cry pierced through the stillness of the woods. It continued on and on like an eerie death wail. Circling above them in the sky, a giant gooney bird swooped up and down above the tree tops.

Ty was shaking. Tears were running down his cheeks. Everyone else had turned pale. Even Jake looked uneasy. Eric threw the stick on the ground by the nest and ran back to join the others.

"Let's get out of here," Jake said.

They moved through the woods, traveling fast. But they couldn't escape the croaking of the gooney bird. It continued to shriek in the sky.

Hurriedly, they shoved off into the next lake at the end of the portage. Each of them was filled with a strange sense of guilt and fear . . . even foreboding.

On the lake, they automatically fell into a fast paddle. It was as though they were racing against something. Jake and Eric's canoe cut through the water in a straight, smooth line. Phil and Pete followed close behind. Ron and Ty struggled to keep up. After two hours of paddling, they were behind, so far behind they were barely in sight of the other two canoes.

"Come on," Ron said nervously to Ty, "hurry it up."

"I'm trying," Ty panted, "I'm trying." But they couldn't narrow the gap between them and the others and they began to feel almost abandoned.

"You don't think Jake would leave us out here, do you?" Ty asked.

"Sure, Jake would," Ron answered. "But Phil wouldn't."

Then they stopped talking. In the sky above them, they heard the flapping of strong wings against the air. Just before it began its dive, the giant gooney bird screamed out its eerie call.

119

The four in the other canoes stopped paddling and turned around. They saw a huge gooney bird diving down, straight down onto Ty and Ron's canoe. Its body was pointing like a finger at their bodies.

They saw Ty cowering low and Ron desperately trying to turn the canoe with his paddle.

At the last second, Ron swung the boat to one side. The gooney bird plunged into the water two feet away. A wave of water almost swamped the canoe. Ty started screaming.

The other two canoes had turned around and were coming toward them. The gooney bird surfaced twenty feet away and then took off again into the air. It had no fish in its beak.

"Ty, shut up," Jake ordered. Ty stopped screaming and stared blankly at Jake.

"We'll stay together from now on," Jake said. Then he swung his canoe around and started off across the lake.

"Are you crazy, Jake?" Phil yelled after him. "Let's turn back. We can get back to where we camped last night."

Jake kept paddling. "I said let's stay together. If you don't get moving, I'll leave you here."

The three canoes moved out across the lake. Ron and Ty paddled mechanically. They couldn't let themselves think of the bird. They couldn't let themselves think at all.

For two more hours they pushed on. This

was a big lake and Jake headed them to its furthest point. Finally, they touched shore on a small island. They pulled their canoes up and waited for Jake's orders.

"We'll head in a ways and see if we can find a decent place to camp."

The six shouldered the canoes and supplies and tramped into the interior of the woods. After ten minutes of walking, they came onto a clearing.

What they saw made them stop short. But no one said a word. No one knew what to say. It was a deserted campsite. Two tents were pitched. A cooking kettle hung over a burnt-out fire. Camping equipment sat around the clearing. It looked as though the people had just disappeared — leaving everything behind.

"I want to get out of here," Ron said.

"Wait a minute . . . wait a minute," Jake repeated as the other five started to go back in the direction from which they came.

"Let's check this place out," Jake said as he walked over to the campfire.

The others sat down the canoes and supplies and walked cautiously over to join Jake.

"Look," Pete said, pointing to some food, "it's only a few days old." Phil kicked a loaf of bread. Insects scurried out of it.

"Why do you think they left?" Ron asked.

No one answered. But each of them, in his head, was thinking of a terrible reason.

"I don't see how they could have left," Phil

said. "I mean, you can't just leave all your supplies out here in the middle of nowhere and then expect to . . ." His voice trailed off; he didn't finish what he was thinking.

"They didn't even take their sleeping bags," Eric said, coming out of one of the tents. "Everything is set up for them to go to bed . . . but they didn't, I guess."

"Come on, you guys, let's get out of here," Ty pleaded.

Jake looked over at Ty's scared face. Then he laughed. "We're not going anywhere. We're camping here tonight."

"No, we're not . . ."

"I want to get out of here . . ."

"This place scares me . . ."

A chorus of five voices broke in on each other, protesting what Jake said.

But Jake had made up his mind. "Pitch the tents," he ordered.

No one, not even Phil, felt secure enough to contradict Jake. Jake was the guide. He was supposed to know this country and these woods. He was the only leader they had.

They pitched their three tents across the clearing from the two empty tents. Jake insisted that they use the same campfire. By the time they were all set up for the night, the sky had begun to grow dark.

Jake lit the sticks of wood he had carefully built up. The wood burst into flame, the yellow tips of fire licking up at the dark night.

The six of them sat around the fire, eating their daily quota of beans, bacon, and stew. There wasn't much conversation. They were all hungry. And their minds were on something they didn't want to talk about.

The night grew darker. Above the high black shadows of the trees, the moon shone in the sky. The campfire was like a beacon light, shining up from the dark woods.

They sat around the fire, still, even though the food had long been eaten. Jake got up from the circle and went down to the lake. The others sat huddled together.

"Do you think we'll be OK, Phil?" Pete asked his brother.

"Sure, Pete." Phil wanted to give some reassurance, some strength. But he felt the same ominous fear that he saw in the others' faces.

"We'll be OK," Ty whispered to himself.

High above them, high up above the towering trees, came the flapping of giant wings. They looked up. The gooney bird passed under the moon. Its black shadow was silhouetted in the moon's silvery light. It began to dive.

The beak was aimed toward the campfire's beacon of light. The beady eyes were fixed upon the circle of bodies in the large clearing. It swooped down on them, making its hoarse call of beckoning to the other giant gooney birds.

It came down in a great swoop over Ty's body. Its strong beak clamped around his neck. Then Ty was pulled upwards, his arms and legs flailing in the wind.

The other giant gooney birds came. Five more giant gooney birds swooped down for their prey.

Moonlight streamed down on the still, deserted campsite.

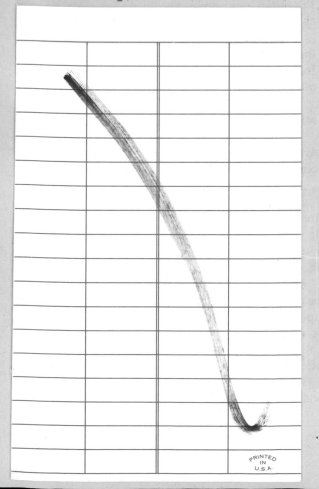

PRINTED
IN
U.S.A.